Fae Reign

Short Story Collection

Judy Lunsford

Fae Reign

Short Story Collection

Judy Lunsford

Introduction

This short story collection is filled with stories written about fae. The stories are filled with fairies, mermaids, changelings, and other fae creatures.

Included in this collection are flash fiction stories as well as much longer stories.

I love writing stories that have a battle between the darkness and the light. Fairies are not always good and usually not to be trusted. But here and there, you may get lucky and stumble upon a fairy that you can rely on.

I hope you find something you like.
Happy reading!

Judy Lunsford
December 2021

We'll kick things off with a short story that I wrote after taking my dog for a walk. It was inspired by some cats that we encountered. Were they really fae in disguise? You make the call.

The Fairy Army

I walk my dog every morning. Right when the sun is showing its first light. Some people call it civil sunrise. It's about a half hour before the actual sunrise.

It's a beautiful time of day. No one else is out, for the most part. And the birds are just waking up and starting to chirp in the trees overhead. The light is just enough to see by, but the sun has not yet risen, so there is no blinding morning light in your eyes as you walk.

Everything looks silver in that light. The world is cast in muted grays and the quiet surrounds you like a cool blanket. The only sounds are the chirping of birds and the occasional grumble of a car starting up.

My dog and I love these morning walks. We both occasionally stop to enjoy the show that the sun puts on each morning, as the yellows and oranges are the first colors that start to bleed into the morning sky. The patterns of the clouds breaking up the pure and uninhibited glow of the first rays of light.

One morning, while we were out on one of our walks, I saw something strange.

We were coming to a corner, where the street turned around a bend, and in the driveway of the house that sits on the outer elbow of the bend was a small figure.

I had to look twice because it was a tiny creature that almost looked like a man, but not quite. He was green skinned and had wings folded up against his back. He was about 12 inches tall, at best. He was dressed as an archer from something out of a Robin Hood type movie. Green tunic and brown pants, with his tunic belted at the waist. He wore a little hat that came to a point in the front. His feet were bare and he stood strongly and proudly in the middle of the empty white driveway. He held a bow at the ready, with a small arrow pointed down the street that went at a right angle from us around the corner.

My dog noticed him first. I wouldn't even have seen the little creature in the dim light if it weren't for my dog. My dog saw him and walked in an interested crouch, staring straight at the little fairy creature.

I followed my dog's line of sight and had to do a double-take when I first saw him. I couldn't believe my eyes. I literally shook my head, trying to clear my vision, and looked again.

The little fairy creature shot his arrow down the street and just moments later, a white and brown calico cat leaped through the air towards him. The arrow was sticking out of the cat's front shoulder, but didn't seem to affect her much.

The little man caught the cat and threw her over his shoulder in an expert judo type throw and the cat landed on her back on the far side of him. He turned towards the cat, ready to face her once again, but the cat thought better of it and skittered away around behind the house.

My dog was rather excited at the sight of the cat, and he was getting restless on the end of his leash. He made a whimpering sound as the cat retreated, which made the fairy creature look up and see us for the first time.

I looked down quickly and shushed my dog, scolding him, "Leave the kitty."

My mind raced as I remembered all of the old warnings I have read about fairies.

One of the things that stuck in my mind at that moment was that you should never let on that you could see fairies. They took being seen by humans badly, and so I made every effort to pretend that I couldn't see the little fairy man.

My dog kept trying to look at him, so I feigned ignorance.

"What are you doing?" I said out loud as we turned the corner and passed the fairy. "The kitty ran away. There's nothing there anymore."

My dog kept looking back, so I said, "No. Leave the kitty alone."

I glanced back over my shoulder as casually as I could and saw that the little man was now following us down the street.

My dog didn't like this, however, and kept trying to turn to face the creature.

"What are you doing?" I scolded. "There's nothing there. The kitty is gone."

I looked back down the street, pretending to look past the fairy, towards where the kitty had wisely retreated.

The fairy motioned to a garden nearby and several more fairies appeared out of bushes and from behind trees and started to follow us.

My dog was becoming more and more agitated, and I had to continue the charade of pretending to not see the crowd of fairies that was now walking down the street behind us.

"Stop it," I said to my dog, straightening him out on the leash. "Let's just go get the mail, you silly dog."

He kept glancing back over his shoulder nervously.

So I boldly turned around and faced the army of fairy creatures that was now behind us. They were in the trees, hopping from branch to branch, and were walking blatantly in the street as well as lurking in the bushes along the front yards behind us.

"What do you keep looking at?" I said. "There's nothing there."

I pretended to look for cats, the way my dog does as he walks, crouching down and peeking under nearby cars.

"See?" I said to my dog. "No kitties."

I tried my best not to seem nervous. It was a struggle to keep my breathing steady as we walked. The hair on the back of my neck was standing up and I could see my dog looking back behind us again and again.

We finally reached the corner to turn to our stack of mailboxes at the side of the road.

"Let's go get the mail," I said cheerfully to my dog.

I glanced around, looking down the street, as if looking for oncoming traffic and could see that there were dozens upon dozens of fairies following us down the street.

There were pretty little ones who flew in the air, and ugly gnomish ones all wrinkled and old looking creeping their way through the bushes that lined the sides of the street. There were more archers in the middle of the street with the first one and several of them had their bows at the ready.

I tried to just casually look around and then up at the birds in the tree above us.

There were even fairies in the trees overhead, staring down at us with curious and menacing faces.

I casually checked the mailbox, which I knew would be empty since I had gotten the mail myself the day before.

"No mail," I said to my dog, who looked up at me nervously. "Are you ready to go home?"

I tried to ignore the arrow that whizzed past us and into the bushes nearby. My dog watched it rattle a nearby bush.

He went over towards the bush and tried to sniff it.

"No," I said. "Leave the birdies alone."

And I pulled on my dog's leash to lead him home.

We made our way around the corner, to our driveway, and inside without incident. But when I looked out the door as it closed, there were fairies lining up all around the front of our house.

I debated for a moment whether or not letting them know where we lived was a good thing or not, but it was too late. And I figured that I would never have been able to lose them or keep up the charade of pretending I couldn't see them for much longer.

I am writing this because I wanted to leave some sort of a record, in case something happens to me.

Because as I write this, there is an army of fairies looking in the window at me. I am still pretending not to see them. And my dog has surrendered enough to just stare at them through the window peacefully. But they are watching my every move.

Originally published in Enchanted Conversation magazine, this story remains a favorite of mine. Part mash-up, part fairy tale of her own, here is a day in the life of a fairy godmother.

The Fairy Godmother

The old woman walked into her garden and breathed in the fresh air. The morning was as perfect as they come. The sun was rising over the horizon into the clearest of clear blue skies. The birds were singing and flitting from branch to branch in the trees that billowed out around the edges above her garden.

She stopped to admire the flowers and the tiny tomatoes and the sage that were peeking up at the early morning sun. She was very pleased at how her garden was coming along.

Her apple tree was filled with shiny red apples that were ready for the picking. She gathered a few and took them inside.

There were many ways to use apples. She had a special order for one in particular.

The Queen of a neighboring kingdom had ordered it herself.

The old woman prepared it in the way that the Queen had asked. Cursed. Poisoned. She hated to do it, but she had bills to pay.

But there were standards to keep.

She made the apple to order, but with a cure. True love's kiss.

It was a longshot, but she had to do something for the poor girl who was going to have to eat the apple. And the extra magic would be undetectable by the Queen. She was a horrible woman anyway, so adding a touch of love would never be noticed through all of the venom and hatred that filled that particular Queen's heart.

She put the apple in a small bundle and took it outside. A large black raven with cloudy white eyes stood on her porch, waiting for the apple. She held up the bundle and the bird dropped a few coins in a small leather bag from his mouth at her feet. She handed him the apple bundle and the bird took it and flew off towards the east and back to the horrible Queen.

It was a terrible thing to need money.

She checked her to-do list and found the next task to be only slightly more to her liking.

She had a request to create a cursed rose, to help to teach a handsome but nasty prince a lesson. It was a task asked for by a friend who had been treated badly by the rude and disdainful prince. She once again made a cure for the curse, by request this time. And once again, true love was the cure.

She sent the rose off to her friend using a rabbit as her messenger. It didn't have far to go to take it to her friend, and she thought it would be nice to get rid of the pesky little fellow for a while. She needed to gather some of the vegetables and herbs from her garden while he was away.

The old woman spent some time in her garden and then some time cleaning up the inside of her house. She wanted things to be in good shape for when she returned home later that evening.

The young girl that she had her eye on needed some help tonight, and it was always lovely to come back home to a clean hearth and home. Especially when it was filled with the wonderful aromas of fresh herbs drying in front of the kitchen window.

When the time came, she gathered the things she needed and headed out to the young girl's house.

When she was sure that the girl's stepmother and stepsisters were gone, she headed inside to talk to the girl.

The old woman found her crying beside the fireplace, all covered with ash and soot.

The old woman sat beside her and spoke encouraging words to the girl. She took her by the hand and led her outside.

It took some creative thinking, but soon a pumpkin was a carriage, some brave mice volunteered to be horses, and the girl's shabby dress became a beautiful ball gown.

The old woman pulled out a pair of glass slippers. Which, of course, was the most important part of the entire evening. She had spent a huge amount of time on them, making sure that the enchantment was exactly right. The shoes had to be a perfect fit, and that kind of magic took time and patience.

The girl was given her instructions and the old woman sent the girl on her way to the ball at the castle. She waved at the carriage as it headed down the road and then dusted off her dress and decided to call it a day.

She was tired from all the magic she had to prepare that day, and she wasn't happy with all of the jobs that had to be done.

She was happy, however, to end the day on a nice note, knowing the sweet and lovely girl would be the one to become the queen of her particular kingdom.

When the old woman went home, the pesky rabbit was already back in her garden, helping himself to a little dinner as a reward for his errand that day. She let him be and headed back inside.

She put a kettle on the fire to make some tea and headed into her bedroom where she found a surprise waiting for her.

A hungry wolf was waiting for her, wearing her nightgown, and moments later, she heard her granddaughter knock on the front door.

It had been a long and busy day, and the old woman decided that she was not going to be eaten by a wolf. She was thoroughly annoyed by the wolf's interruption, so she used her magic to change the wolf into a cat and picked him up and carried him out the back door.

She tossed the wolf, who was now a cat, into the pig pen with her three piglets and went back inside to answer the door.

It had been a while since she had seen her granddaughter, and she had a beautiful red cloak waiting for her.

What would you do if you discovered that you were inadvertently living someone else's life? Can a changeling ever go back?

Marigold & Elfie

Marigold woke up with a start and kicked the blankets off herself almost immediately. The sun was already coming in through the window and streaming down into her room in bright lines from between the half open shutters. The little prismed globes that she had hanging on different length pieces of fishing line in her window cast hundreds of rainbows around her room and sparkled in the sunlight.

Her mother was already up and downstairs. She could tell by the fact that the cupboards were being slammed shut in the kitchen. It was the familiar sounds of her mother making breakfast.

When Marigold was a small child, she used to flinch when loud noises occurred around the house, but now the loud noises were totally normal, even comforting for her. It meant the presence of her family. It meant people were home. It meant the ones she loved were safe and happy.

Her parents and both of her older brothers were all Deaf. Everyone in the family was except for her.

She had always felt like an outcast in the family, even though no one ever treated her that way. Even her brothers, with all the teasing and torture that older brothers do, never made her feel like she didn't belong.

Marigold was excited this morning because the snow had melted the day before and, it being a weekend, she would be allowed to go for a walk in the woods once again.

It didn't snow much where she lived, but when it did, her mother wouldn't let Marigold out of the house.

Marigold had been a sickly child. There were lots of visits to the hospital all throughout her childhood. Lots of tests that were run and lots of doctors scratching their heads unhelpfully and not coming up with any answers. And the doctors never seemed to try very hard.

Her mother became frustrated because she felt that since they were Deaf, it was too troublesome for many of the doctors to bother to even try to communicate with them.

But with time, and loving care from her family, Marigold had grown up healthy and strong. All thanks to her mother, and very little thanks to doctors. Her mother learned on her own what she needed to know and took care of Marigold until she was strong and healthy.

Marigold was small for her age. She always had been. But otherwise, her health had recovered, except in the eyes of her worried mother.

Her mother had become overly protective of Marigold's well-being, as any mother would be, and hated for Marigold to be out in bad weather. She always worried about Marigold getting sick again and lived in a constant state of anxiety about her health.

After breakfast, Marigold signed to her mother that she was going out for a walk.

A brief argument ensued and ended with her mother making her put on a heavier coat and an extra scarf, just in case, before letting Marigold leave the house.

It was the day before Valentine's Day, so Marigold's mother had chosen a bright red scarf and waved it at Marigold before she left and signed for her to put it on.

Marigold relented as her mother tied the red scarf around her neck, over the top of the pretty sparkling purple one that she already wore and gave her a kiss on the cheek.

Marigold rolled her eyes at her mother, waved goodbye, and headed out the door.

On the other side of her family's back fence was a beautiful forest.

Marigold had always loved going for walks in the forest. She felt more at home there than she ever had anywhere else.

She loved her family dearly, but she always felt like an outsider. Like she didn't belong. And not because she wasn't Deaf. It was something deeper. Something that called her to the woods while her family was happy to stay at home.

Marigold made her way through the trees, marveling at the sight of the empty naked branches as they danced happily in the breeze.

She loved the feeling of the warm morning sun as it kissed her face and the sound of the birds rustling around on the ground as they scratched around and looked for food.

She went to her favorite spot, where a group of trees stood mysteriously in a circle. All the rest of the trees in the forest were so randomly placed. But this grove always seemed so intentional.

In the center of the circle was an old stump. The tree that had been cut down had been very large and was in the exact center of the circle of trees.

Marigold stared at the stump and thought once again what a shame it was to have such a majestic tree cut down in the middle of such a perfect grove.

She sat down on the stump and pulled a book out of her pocket. She sat, reading in the morning sunlight, shivering slightly when the wind blew hard enough to cut through the layers of her jacket.

Marigold was secretly glad her mother had made her wear the extra scarf, even though she would never tell her mother anything of the sort.

Marigold enjoyed the morning and sat on her stump and read until something suddenly blocked the sunlight.

She looked up, expecting to see more winter storm clouds moving across the sky, but instead, she saw a girl about her age, fifteen or sixteen, standing over her and staring down, looking at her curiously.

She was wearing an old torn light blue dress that couldn't possibly be warm enough for the time of year and she looked strikingly like Marigold herself.

Marigold stood up and looked at the girl. It was like looking in a mirror, except for the fact that the girl was an inch or so taller.

She had the same light brown, kinky coily curls that Marigold did. But her hair was a mess, with tangles and matted clumps about her messy hair.

The same brown eyes stared back at her. The girl's eyes were filled with curiosity and confusion.

Marigold felt like she was looking in a very messy, very dirty mirror.

"Come back," a voice called from the far side of the circle of trees.

Marigold looked around the girl and into the trees.

The girl didn't react to the voice at all.

A small fairy burst through the trees and flew towards the center of the circle, but she came to a screeching halt when she saw Marigold standing in front of the girl.

"Oh, my goddess," the fairy said. She slapped her hands to her cheeks and stared at Marigold as she peeked around the other girl.

"Elfie?" the fairy whispered. "Is that really you?"

"I'm sorry, who?" Marigold said.

The fairy was no taller than the length of Marigold's arm and her skin glowed the palest blue in the sunlight. She had raven black hair that fell down her back in long tresses intertwined with slim twigs from the branches of some plant or other.

"I can't believe it," the fairy said. "You're still alive? But how?"

"Who are you?" Marigold asked, stunned by the creature flitting about in front of her.

"I'm Tansy," the fairy said. "I'm not surprised that you don't remember me."

"We've met before?" Marigold's eyebrows shot up in surprise.

"Sort of," Tansy said. "I was your carrier."

"What's a carrier?" Marigold asked.

Tansy looked sheepish and glanced back and forth between Marigold and the almost identical girl in front of her.

"You're a changeling," Tansy said. "Or really, you were born a fairy, can't you feel it?"

Marigold looked at the cloudless sky above her and at the circle of trees. She thought about the way the forest and the outdoors in general called to her. And about how she never felt truly at home anywhere within the world of people.

Even in the tight knit Deaf Community, who treated her as one of their own, she felt different and out of place. Something that other hearing children of Deaf parents claimed they didn't feel in that community. It was a wonderful family of caring people that accepted her unconditionally.

But she still always felt the call of the outdoors. Away from people of any sort. At home in the trees and among the flowers. The rippling of the summer grass seemed to call out to her, and the wind whispered her name.

"You know I'm right," Tansy said. "I can see it in your eyes."

"Why was I a changeling?" she asked.

Marigold had heard legends of fairies who had been left in the cribs of stolen babies. She was familiar with the concept from the many books she read.

"You were weak and sickly," Tansy said. "It broke your poor mother's heart. So, we switched you with a human baby to console her."

"So, this girl really belongs with my family?" Marigold pointed at the filthy teen who glanced back and forth between them as she and Tansy talked.

"It didn't work," Tansy said. "The girl can't hear, so your mother rejected her as a replacement."

"Why didn't you trade her back?" Marigold asked. "Put her back where she belonged? Take me away again so she could have her life back?"

"By the time we figured it out, it was too late," Tansy said.

"What happened to my mother?" Marigold asked.

"She wept herself into a terrible melancholy,"
Tansy said sadly. "And she died of a broken heart."

"And my father?" Marigold asked.

Tansy shrugged, "We don't even know who he is."

"Does she speak?" Marigold asked. "Or sign?"

"No," Tansy said. "Never a word."

Marigold took a deep breath. She looked at the girl standing beside her.

"How did you let her get so filthy?" Marigold asked.

Tansy shrugged, "She's wild, unpredictable. And she hates having a bath. So, we let her be."

"And you watch her?" Marigold asked.

"Yes," Tansy nodded. "I was assigned to take her on as my responsibility, since I was the one who chose the wrong house. But honestly, the older she gets the more tiresome she becomes."

"How can you say that?" Marigold could feel the anger rising in her chest. "She's a human being and she has rights. And needs love, and a proper home."

"Then give her yours," Tansy said.

"What?" Marigold was stunned by the suggestion. "I can't, I mean just look at her. And I love my family. I can't just leave them."

"All excuses," Tansy waved her hand at Marigold. "If you want to put things right, you can. By giving her back her home. It would solve my problems and I could have my life back as well."

"How would she be able to go back?" Marigold asked. "She doesn't know sign language. She doesn't know her parents. You've stolen away her life, her language, and her family. How can she possibly go back now? What would explain the hearing loss? And the memory loss?"

"You could use your magic," Tansy said.

Marigold scoffed. "I have no magic."

"Just because you've never used it, doesn't mean you don't have any," Tansy said.

"I have no magic," Marigold repeated.

"Look around you," Tansy said. "Do you really think these trees just grew this way? This is where you come, right? I can feel your magic all around us."

"I didn't do this," Marigold said.

Tansy looked around at the trees, "Yes, you did. I can tell."

Marigold looked at the girl, who was watching her carefully as she wound her fingers through Marigold's curls.

"I'm so sorry," Marigold signed to the girl.

She looked at Marigold with confusion, not understanding the meaning of the gestures.

Marigold let the girl feel the softness of her hair and let her stare intently into her own brown eyes.

"She knows you have her life," Tansy said. "You can give it back to her. It is in your power."

"What would I have to do?" Marigold asked, not able to tear her eyes away from the brown ones looking back at her.

"You have to give up your life to her," Tansy said. "She will have all of your memories. She won't have any memory loss. She will remember two lives. She'll know your languages. She will fit in just fine. The only thing she won't have is her hearing."

"That honestly wouldn't be that hard to explain," Marigold said. "As long as she has all of my memories. Doctors wouldn't be able to figure it out, but they never figured out what was wrong with me in the first place."

"Because they can't diagnose a fairy," Tansy said. "Our anatomy is very similar, but not our biology."

"What would happen to me?" Marigold asked.

"You would cease to be," Tansy said. "Except in her memories, of course. But you were left to die anyway. So really, it would just be setting everything right again, wouldn't it?"

"How can you be so callous?" Marigold snapped.

"I'm a fairy," Tansy shrugged. "Death is just a part of the natural lifecycle. If you feel so strongly about her being stolen, then you should only feel that it's natural for you to give up your life for hers. That's the way it was meant to be in the first place. She lives, you die."

"What will happen to her if I refuse?" Marigold asked.

"Then she will die," Tansy said. "I came to set her free. She is barely surviving the winters now. And she's gotten too big to stay in my house. So, she must go. Maybe it was fate that brought us here, to you. It's within your power to save her."

Marigold could feel the weight of two lives crashing down on her.

"And if you choose not to," Tansy said. "You will receive her lifeforce when she dies. And you will live forever."

Marigold didn't feel right about having stolen the life of this girl who was standing before her. And the thought of living forever felt daunting and lonely.

"How do I-?" Marigold looked to ask Tansy another question, but the fairy was gone.

Marigold sighed.

"Let's at least get you cleaned up," Marigold said.

She put out her hand and the other girl took it.

Marigold led her home and waited for the house to be empty.

When her parents were off to work, and her brothers were off to friends' houses, she snuck the girl into the house and brought her upstairs to clean her up.

After a long fight and many tantrums, Marigold was able to do a reasonable job in cleaning the girl up. The bathroom was a filthy mess, but that was the least of Marigold's concerns.

The more time she spent with the girl, the more she felt that the right thing to do was to give her back the life that she had stolen. No matter how much she would miss it herself.

Marigold gave the girl the clothes she was wearing, so that when her mother came home, the girl would be dressed like Marigold was when her mother last saw her. The only thing she kept was the red scarf.

Marigold quickly dressed in some old clothes from the back of her closet and came back to the girl who was now admiring the warm clothes she now wore.

She looked into the mirror as the two of them stood side by side and Marigold could see that the girl was getting stronger and that her own reflection was starting to fade away, just a little around the edges.

"It looks like if we stay together long enough, the magic will just happen," Marigold said.

The girl looked at her and smiled.

"Come on," Marigold put her hand out to the girl once again. "If we're going to do this, let me say goodbye."

Marigold went around the house and looked one last time at the pictures of her family that hung on the walls. Of Marigold's family. Of the family that belonged to the girl who stood beside her and who reached out to touch the pictures gently with her fingertips. She was seeing her family for the first time and didn't even realize it. Not yet anyways.

Marigold led the other Marigold back outside and they went back to the perfect circle of trees. She looked up at the sky one last time.

She stepped up onto the stump in the middle of the clearing and listened to the wind whistle through the trees. She watched the clouds move across the sky. And she could smell the fact that spring would be coming soon.

She reached out her hand to the girl and pulled her up onto the stump. They stood face to face and the girl stared down at her.

"You take good care of them," Marigold signed to the girl.

She just smiled in return.

Marigold took the red scarf from around her neck and placed it around the girl's and tied it, just the way their mother did.

"Have a happy Valentine's Day, okay?" Marigold signed.

The girl just looked at her with a slight frown.

"You'll know what that means in a minute."

They joined hands and Marigold looked up at the sky.

When she looked down, she was facing the opposite direction. The Marigold who could hear was gone. The only one to remain was the real Marigold. The Deaf Marigold. The complete Marigold.

She looked around and saw that the sky was getting dark.

She knew she needed to get home.

The complete Marigold looked around at the perfect circle of trees and the sky above her.

She could still feel the call of nature around her. But it wasn't as strong as the fairy part of her remembered it.

She climbed down off the stump and started on her way home.

Marigold could remember everything clearly. From both lives.

She looked back behind her and realized that she hadn't even noticed the silence that now surrounded her.

It was comforting.

It would take some explaining. Or not.

She could leave that to the already frustrated doctors.

Marigold took one last look at the circle of trees. The stump in the center had become a majestic oak tree, towering above the other trees, and already starting to show the first tiny leaf buds of spring.

It was no longer a sawed-off stump sticking out of the ground.

Marigold went back to the tree and took off her red scarf. She tied it around the magnificent trunk and stood back to look at the towering new addition to the circle of trees.

The circle was now complete as well.

She placed a hand on the trunk of the tree and then signed, "Thank you."

She took one last look at the grove around her. She could feel the love that surrounded her, coming from the circle of trees.

She knew she would be back, just not quite as often as she used to come. The fairy memories in her didn't need it anymore.

Marigold headed back home to explain things to her family.

She didn't know how she would explain her sudden hearing loss. But she knew it didn't matter. She knew they would love her, no matter what.

The fairy magic in her was gone. She could feel that loss, all the magic she never knew was there was now buried deep in the oak tree. The lifecycle of the fairy was complete and set right again.

And for the lost Marigold, it was finally time for her to feel complete.

It was finally time to go home.

Icarus dreamed of a different life. A better life. Could the butterflies actually take him there?

THE BUTTERFLY BOY

Icarus always thought he had an unfortunate name. His mother loved mythology and named each of her children, and pets, after her favorite mythological characters.

After four brothers, two sisters, six dogs, three cats, a bird, a lizard, sixteen goldfish, and a turtle, his mother was running low on the good names. So, Icarus it was.

He wouldn't have minded it so badly, except for the fact that the kids at school called him Icky, among other things. So did his brothers for that matter. His sisters did as well, but only when they were angry with him.

He also didn't like the fact that his name wasn't borrowed from a hero, but from someone to not be like. Many times, Icarus pictured his namesake falling from the sky after disobeying his father and flying too close to the sun. He was named after someone who was doomed.

Unlike his namesake, Icarus kept to the shadows. He wanted to hide from the ones who called him Icky. Icarus preferred not to be seen.

When the other children were playing on the playground, Icarus would find a place far away from the other children. He usually either quietly read, or he laid on his back with his arms behind his head and watched the clouds move across the sky.

Icarus wasn't sure exactly when the butterflies first started coming.

The first one came by itself, so did the second, and the third, and so on. They were just part of the scenery. Part of the peace that came from being alone. Sometimes he noticed them, sometimes he didn't. It was when they came in a small swarm that Icarus finally really took notice.

He was laying in the grass one day, at the farthest end of the soccer field. He found that he was usually safe out behind the farthest goal net. The bullies who called him Icky didn't like to walk out that far just to get their kicks. They settled on kids that stayed closer to the playground. Just like animals in the wild, they stalked the easier prey.

Icarus could hear them in the distance. It was Eugene's turn today. A boy with another unfortunate name. Icarus felt bad for Eugene, but he tried to block out the badness of the world when he was out this far.

Icarus felt the blades of grass tickle his arms and his ears. He shifted around a little bit until he became more comfortable. The smell of freshly cut grass was sharp to his nose and he decided he liked the strong smell, even though he felt like the cuttings were stuck in his throat. The grass was also slightly damp from the early morning sprinklers, but in the moment he didn't care.

Icarus stared up at the sky and made a game out of naming what each cloud looked like. He saw a tiger, a giraffe, and a Volkswagen bug move slowly and gracefully across his view.

While he was trying to decide if a certain cloud looked more like a horse or a train, he saw a swarm of butterflies flit above him. It was the fact that there were so many of them that caught his attention. He had never seen so many at once. He rolled over in the grass as they flew past and across the field, so that he could keep them in view.

They were the most beautiful thing he had ever seen. The orange and black of their wings flitting wildly against the blue sky. They seemed so graceful and chaotic as they flew across the field and flitted up the hill and disappeared over the high wall that led to one of the houses in the neighborhood that bordered the school.

Once they were out of sight, Icarus felt happy. He felt like he just saw something wondrous. Something that was meant just for him and was all his own. Something he didn't have to share with classmates or siblings. The butterflies came for him.

He heard the bell off in the distance that signified that recess was over. He sat up and went to gather up his book and his jacket. Icarus looked down at his shorts and suddenly realized with a shock that laying on freshly cut wet grass might not have been the best idea.

The back of his shorts were covered in green stains. He reached around and pulled his shirt by the shoulder to try to get a look at the back of his shirt, but he couldn't see it. So, he pulled his arms into his sleeves and spun his shirt around. He looked down to see that the back of his light-yellow shirt was completely stained with grass green blotches.

Icarus sighed and turned his shirt back around. He pulled on his jacket, over the grass stains, and tried to pull it down as far as he could over the back of his shorts. It wouldn't reach far enough, so deciding shirt stains were better than stains on the back of his shorts, he pulled off his jacket and tied it around his waist.

He picked up his book and started to jog back across the soccer field and back to class. He realized that he was going to be late if he didn't hurry. And the last thing he wanted was to have all eyes on him when he walked into the classroom late, and covered with wet green stains.

Icarus suffered through the rest of the day. The laughing, the jeers, the other students calling him Icky Sticky. The bullies were waiting to taunt him and push him down into the grass out in front of the school so that he would have matching grass stains on the front of his clothes. The day went past in a blur to Icarus.

What got him through were the butterflies.

They were all he could think about. As he lay on the grass face down, with the foot of one of the bullies grinding down in the center of his back, his mind went blank, except for the butterflies. He was out on the field again, watching the swarm flit across the blue background of the spring sky. They danced around him and showed off their majestic orange markings. Even after the bullies left to go home, Icarus stayed on the ground and imagined the butterflies coming again just for him.

Once at home, the butterflies were all he could think about. He spent the evening researching butterflies. He ignored his homework and studied everything he could find about them.

The next day, Icarus came prepared. He had put a small picnic blanket in his backpack. His mother kept it in the hall closet, way in the back. He had to stand on the bottom shelf to reach it, pushing all of the old towels and rags out of the way to dig back into the very back where he remembered it being hidden.

It was perfect. Red and white checkered pattern on the top, a plastic protective layer sewn to the bottom. It was smashed oddly from being in the back of the linen closet. But Icarus smuggled it into the basement, where he had a small reading corner all to himself. His siblings didn't like the basement, so they left him alone when he was down there. He knew he was safe to spread out the blanket, smooth it out the best he could, and then refold it as neatly as a plastic blanket would fold to fit into his backpack with all of his books and supplies.

The bullies couldn't bother him that morning. At least he thought they couldn't.

But they were merciless. The cool spring morning had covered the grass with a coating of dew, and the gardeners still hadn't adjusted the sprinklers out on the field. As Icarus headed out towards the soccer field at recess, the bullies stopped him just before he could set foot on the grass.

Icarus stood on the graying asphalt, looking down at the ground where the cracked and crumbling asphalt gave way to the muddy edge of the grassy field.

He tuned out their insults and jeers, and when he gave them no reaction, they shoved him down into the mud.

Icarus landed with a splash and he felt the cold slimy mud squish through his fingers. His arms weren't ready for the impact, so his chest splashed down into the cold wet muddy puddle, drenching his shirt to his skin. The grit of the mud crunched between his teeth as he tried to spit his mouth clear.

The other boys laughed and left him there to pull himself out of the mud. His shirt was darkened and his bare arms were coated with muck.

He crawled over to the grass and stood up on sturdier ground. He held his arms away from himself and looked at his mud-covered clothes.

Icarus watched as the bullies walked away, guffawing and slapping each other on the back, occasionally turning to point and laugh at Icarus. He stood there, dripping with mud in the sunshine, spitting a seemingly endless supply of mud and grit into the grass.

Icarus wanted nothing more than to go home, change his clothes, and crawl back under the covers and go back to sleep. He wanted to pretend this day had never happened. He wanted to be dry. He didn't want to go back to his classroom covered in mud. In fact, he didn't want to go back at all. The title of Icky Sticky would cement itself to Icarus when he went back. Something he didn't feel he could ever live down. Too many of his other classmates had caught on to it the day before.

But then he remembered his goal. The butterflies.

Icarus pulled out a towel he had packed in his backpack with his picnic blanket. He had thought to pack it just in case. He wished that he had thought to pack an extra shirt. He was able to use the towel to wipe the mud off of his face and most of it from his arms, but by that time it was too damp and muddy to even attempt to fix his shirt.

Icarus left the towel on the ground at the edge of the mud puddle, picked up his backpack, and headed to the far end of the soccer field. When he got there, he spread out his picnic blanket on the ground behind the soccer net.

He looked at his arms, which were still streaked with mud, and sighed. He laid down on his red and white checked picnic blanket and stared up at the sky. The clouds were fewer and farther between that day. And the wind didn't blow them across the sky. They sat high up in the air, like big cotton balls spilled from a bag.

His muddy shirt stuck to his chest; a cold layer of wet filth pressed against him that reminded him of why he hid out in the depths of the soccer field.

He shut his eyes, just for a moment, to soak in the warmth of the sun. He wanted to forget the chill of the mud and the shrieking laughter of the bullies. The warmth of the sun felt good. He could feel the mud drying and the world slipping away.

When he opened his eyes, they were there. The butterflies hovered above him, flitting gracefully and wildly against the blue sky and white cotton that hung above them.

He lifted his arm and held his hand out to the butterflies. One of them flitted towards him and landed on his outstretched hand. He brought it closer to his face and watched as the beautiful orange and black winged creature slowly opened and closed its wings as it perched on his index finger. Icarus could see the delicate pattern of the bright orange dots on the creature's wings.

He wished he could be part of their orange and black kaleidoscope, flitting about in the spring sunshine.

Icarus laid back on his blanket and stared up at the other butterflies. They stayed close, not wanting to leave their friend. Icarus held his hand gently and let the butterfly sit on his finger for as long as it liked.

It was peaceful. Icarus wished he could stay like that forever. Laying on the grass, with a butterfly perched on his finger. Watching the kaleidoscope of the other butterflies flitting happily above him against the dappled white and vivid blue sky.

Icarus could hear shouts off in the distance. He tore his eyes away from the butterflies and saw that the bullies were heading across the field towards him.

He started to panic. The last thing he wanted was for the bullies to invade his safe place and see the butterflies. They weren't something he was ready to share with anyone, especially not them.

"You have to fly away now," he told the butterfly that was nestled on his finger.

It answered him by slowly flapping its wings.

The other butterflies came down from the sky. They swarmed around Icarus and each took a place at the edge of his red and white checked picnic blanket.

The butterflies lifted the edges of the blanket and Icarus could feel himself rising up off the ground. He laid back in the blanket to balance himself and let the butterflies lift him up, high above the soccer field.

Icarus could hear the bullies shouting below him, but they couldn't reach him.

The butterflies carried Icarus high into the sky. He kept his eyes on the butterflies flitting wildly against the blue sky as they carried him off to where the butterflies go. Somewhere safe from the bullies. Somewhere where it was acceptable to be covered in mud.

The butterflies flew high, but they kept Icarus from flying too close to the sun. And Icarus knew that the kaleidoscope of tiny little wings would never let him fall.

THE REPLACEMENT

No one asked what happened to the butterfly boy. The child who was whisked away by a kaleidoscope of Monarch butterflies one day during recess. He had brought a red and white checked picnic blanket to school with him, to protect himself from the cold mud and wet grass as he laid on the ground at the farthest end of the soccer field and watched the clouds drift by.

The butterflies came in a swarm of dancing orange and black and carried him off to protect him from the bullies that were coming for him. To do him harm.

There were a few whispers here and there about what may have been seen that day, but no one dared to speak of it out loud. To say that you witnessed a child being kidnapped by a kaleidoscope of butterflies would make you an object of ridicule, wouldn't it?

Especially since his mother didn't even notice he was gone.

But that was only because the changeling child replaced him so seamlessly.

He looked just like the butterfly boy, an exact duplicate in every way. The only difference was a birthmark on his shoulder. Some said it actually looked like a butterfly.

But the changeling boy was different.

He didn't let the bullies get away with beating him up. He was strong. When one of the bullies tried to shove him down into the mud, the changeling boy turned the tables on the bully. And for the first time, the bully tasted the mud that he shoved so many other children down into. He didn't even know how he got there, his mouth full of muck and grit. But when the changeling boy was finished with him, that bully didn't feel like bullying other children anymore.

Eventually, the changeling boy grew up. He never fit in with his peers. He stayed in the shadows, away from everyone else. But he always acted as a guardian to the ones who were bullied.

I watched him from the secret corners and dark shadows that allowed me a view into his world. He was always an oddity, but he lived my life better than I ever did. Of course, I was a child when he took my place. Still in elementary school. I never had much of a chance to live.

It was years before I knew a changeling had taken my place. I was raised by the butterflies that had absconded with me. And the fairies that lived with them. They had been my family for years. I was happy. But the fairies had me under a spell.

It wasn't until there was an accident in the forest one night that the spell was broken. There had been a terrible thunderstorm, and the fairy that had cast my spell was hit by lightning. She was killed instantly, and just as fast, the spell that had me in their thrall was broken.

The shock of realizing how many years I had lost came slowly. Especially since I didn't even know what year it was, or how old I was for that matter. Fairies didn't usually keep track of things that way.

All I knew was that I needed to find my family. I had been gone for years; I thought my mother would be devastated. Imagine my surprise when I went to my childhood home and not only was my family still there, but so was I.

I had heard of changelings from the whispers among the butterflies. But they didn't like to answer my questions about them and while under the fairy's spell, they could change the subject without much argument from me.

I watched the changeling with my family through the window each night. They had no idea he wasn't really me. Most of my older brothers and sisters had moved out. He, I was around sixteen, and was the youngest of seven. So, my family had gotten much smaller. Just my mother, the changeling, and two of my older brothers sat down to dinner each night. The rest, presumably, were in college or out on their own by then.

It broke my heart and spurred on my anger as I realized how much I had lost. I didn't even know where to find my other siblings.

I had to make things right. I had to take my life back.

One night, I went out into the tool shed and found an old pair of pruning shears. They were very old and a bit rusty, but still sharp.

I went back out to the back window where I had been watching my family have dinner with the imposter. They were inside, cleaning up. The changeling was at the sink washing dishes while my mother was still clearing the table. My brothers were busying themselves with not helping, making me realize that some things never change.

I stood just outside the window, in the shadows. I didn't want my mother to see. But I did want him to see.

The changeling boy looked up and he did see me. Our eyes locked and I motioned for him to come outside.

He said something to my mother and dried his hands. He went to the back door. I waited for him just outside. I stayed hidden and ready.

I caught him off guard. It was easier to kill him than I thought it would be. And just when I was trying to decide what to do with the body, he faded away and disappeared. Like he never was.

I waited for my mother to go upstairs, and then I snuck inside. I cleaned up and changed into some fresh clothing, the first I'd had in years.

I knew I wouldn't fit in at first, with all the time I had lost. I never had fit in. I never had the chance.

But now, finally, I had the chance to try. I had stolen back my life. The butterfly boy was home.

Pooka Deals

Sometimes Quinn Albright hated her job. When she had decided to become a PI, she thought it would be fun, maybe even exciting.

Instead, she wound up working for an investment company to pay the bills. Her job was to perform due diligence before the company invested in anything new. It was her job to make sure that there was no fraud being committed and that the investment wasn't some sort of a Ponzi scheme.

She was a paper pusher.

And she hated it.

But not tonight.

Tonight, her most recent case led her to a Mr. Noah Larson.

The problem was, he was supposed to be dead.

But here she was, out in the middle of the night, trailing Mr. Larson to the edge of town.

He had left a lot of money to the company she worked for when he died.

She had first heard about it through the rumor mill, but thought nothing of it until her boss called her into his office and asked her to find Mr. Larson.

"I'm sorry," she said. "Isn't he the guy that died?"

She was sitting in Mr. Nguyen's office. He had the best office on the floor, as far as Quinn was concerned. It was a corner office, with a view of the city out not one wall, but two. One side even had a view that overlooked the river.

Mr. Nguyen had his desk strategically placed so that he could see the river and his door from where he sat. But Quinn, in the chair in front of his desk, could see neither.

She didn't have to go in there very often. But when she did, it made her very nervous. Mr. Nguyen never saw anyone unless it was something major. And he usually fired people who did unsatisfactory work.

"Yes, he is the man who left us a lot of money in a trust. He requested that we consider distributing the money to various charitable organizations," Mr. Nguyen said. "But we suspect he's still alive. And if he is, we don't want to accept any of this money. It could lead to lawsuits that we don't care to deal with. I want you to make sure that he is dead. And if he's not, find out what he's up to and why he wanted us to take his money."

"Is there a reason that he chose this company to be his executor?" Quinn asked.

"If you happen to find him, maybe you can ask him that too," Mr. Nguyen said. "He has no connection to the company that we know of, no reason that we can see that he would choose us to make those financial decisions for him. Especially since he has family. Distant kin, but still family according to the law."

He handed Quinn the file. She flipped through it and looked up at her boss.

"I know this is unusual," Mr. Nguyen said. "But you're our top investigator. Your recommendations have been on the mark every single time. So, I'm confident you can do this."

Quinn thanked Mr. Nguyen, took the folder, and left his office.

She flipped through the file as she walked down the beige hallway and back to her office. With her single window that had a view of the building across the way.

Quinn racked her brain as she tried to think of where to start looking for a dead man.

She sat down in front of the laptop she kept in her office and brought up all the information she could find on Mr. Larson.

He led a fairly normal life. He worked at an investment firm, not unlike her own. He had been an associate, well on his way up the corporate ladder when he suddenly retired early last year.

He had no wife, no children, his parents had passed away years ago. The only family he had were cousins that he didn't really seem to have anything to do with.

Quinn checked his social media pages online. He only had professional links and very little was posted that wasn't about his professional life. His social media activity ended when he retired. There was no other sign of him online.

She checked his credit history and criminal record. He was clean. Boring. Just an average guy who focused his entire life on his work because he really didn't have much else.

Quinn stared at the screen wondering what it was that had made him retire early.

She looked at his credit history. The last major purchase he had made on his credit card was a trip to the Caribbean. Which he had fully paid off, she noted. He retired shortly after his trip.

She also noticed in the file that his funeral was the following day. She figured that was as good of a place to start as any and planned to attend.

She figured, who would want to miss their own funeral?

*

The following day, Quinn dressed in black. She made sure she was wearing low heeled shoes because it was going to be a graveside service. She didn't want to spend the afternoon pulling her heels out of the grass.

She hovered near the back, so she could watch things clearly. She was curious to see who would show up. This man had no close family, and hadn't worked in over a year.

She was right when she figured it would be a very low turnout. And of the few who came, not one shed a tear for the man.

It was a closed casket, so she had no idea if he was really in the casket that was being lowered into the ground, and she couldn't think of a good reason to ask the mortuary if they would open it for her before the ceremony.

She was getting ready to leave when she noticed a dark shadow off to her left. She turned to look and saw a man skulking around behind a tree, watching the memorial service from a distance.

The man matched Mr. Larson's approximate weight and height.

Quinn needed to get a closer look to be sure.

She tilted her head away from the man and headed back to her car, hoping he wouldn't take notice of her as the casket was being lowered into the ground.

Quinn circled back from the parking area and tried to get a better look at the man.

As far as she could tell, he was Noah Larson. He looked just like the pictures she had seen of him online.

He put on a pair of sunglasses and pulled his hat lower down over his face and headed to his car.

Quinn raced back to her car, determined to follow him.

She tried to remember everything she had learned about how to tail someone. It had been a long since she had last done it. She was sure she was following too close, in hopes of not losing his vehicle in traffic.

He got onto the highway and headed south.

She knew she could follow him at a much larger distance on the highway, but she wondered where he was headed.

She was sure this was the right guy.

Quinn started getting nervous as his car headed across the state line. She called into work and left a message for Mr. Nguyen that she was fairly sure that she had found Mr. Larson and was currently following his vehicle south on the interstate.

Her assistant checked the license plate number for her and verified that it was a rental.

"Be careful," her assistant had said before hanging up. "I have a bad feeling that this guy doesn't want to be found for a reason."

"Then he shouldn't have gone to his own funeral," Quinn said.

They drove for hours, only stopping occasionally for gas. Quinn tried to stop at alternate gas stations or park at opposite ends of the lot when they stopped.

At one rest stop, he had left while she was still in the bathroom, and it was several miles of panicking and driving over the speed limit before she caught up to him again.

She wondered if he had noticed her following him at this point. They had been driving the same route, making the same stops all day.

She kept up the ruse and was glad that she had thought to bring more comfortable clothes with her to change out of after the funeral. But she had yet to do so.

They drove into the night, and Quinn hoped and prayed that she would stay awake while driving. It had been a long day and they had travelled through several states. It was much harder to follow someone in the dark. She only hoped that she was still following the right set of tail lights in the darkness.

When they finally crossed the state line into Louisiana, Quinn was fairly sure they were headed to New Orleans. What she didn't know was why.

She wondered if there was some connection to his trip to the Caribbean that changed the direction of his life and now brought him here to New Orleans.

Quinn followed Larson to the French Quarter, where he parked his car and set out on foot. She parked her car, and was glad that she hadn't had time to change out of her funeral outfit, with the exception of her shoes, and set out on foot after him.

She followed him for quite a way. He never looked behind him to see if he was being followed. He seemed to be walking with a singular focus.

He walked off the main well-lit street and down a darker side street. It was much sleepier than the main-street where a few establishments were still open and tourists enjoyed the late-night life.

But as they went deeper down the unlit side street, it got quieter and much more ominous in the darkness.

She quietly crept along behind him, fairly sure that he had no idea she was still there.

He went around a corner and into an alley between two dark buildings. When Quinn got there, she could see two doors in the alley, and a wall at the end with no other exit. Mr. Larson was gone.

She stood between the two doors, looking back and forth between them. Quinn figured she had a fifty-fifty chance of picking the right door, so she chose the blue one.

It was locked.

She turned and looked at the green one, took a deep breath and tried the knob.

It was locked as well.

"Crap," she muttered to herself.

She still didn't know which door to pick.

But it didn't matter, because Mr. Larson came out of the shadows and slammed her up against the brick wall beside the green door. He held his arm against her throat so tightly that it lifted her a few inches, leaving her scrambling to keep her toes on the ground.

"Why are you following me?" he demanded.

"Mr. Larson?" she hoped using his name would calm him down, but it only seemed to make him angrier.

"Who sent you?" he demanded, slamming her against the wall even harder.

Cornered and being threatened in a dark alley, Quinn decided that the truth was her best course of action.

"My boss," Quinn said, gasping for breath. "Mr. Nguyen, he didn't believe you were dead."

Larson almost laughed; he loosened his hold against her slightly. "This is about the money?"

Quin just nodded as best as she could, too scared to find any more words.

Larson released her completely and she lowered herself back down onto her feet.

Every part of her being wanted to send a knee hard into his groin, but since she needed answers, she held herself in check.

"You can tell your boss that the money is his, free and clear," Larson laughed again. "Where I'm going, I will have no need for money."

"Where are you going?" she asked, rubbing her throat with one hand.

"I can't tell you," he said. "But as far as this world is concerned, I'm as good as dead."

"What do you mean?' she asked.

Larson started walking back up the alley towards the street.

"Stop following me," he said over his shoulder.

Quinn had to almost jog to keep up with him.

"I can't go back until I have some answers," she said. "My boss will never take the money if he knows that you're alive."

"Then don't tell him," Larson said. "I need him to take that money."

"Why?" Quinn was thoroughly confused. "Where is it that you are going?"

A large man stepped out from another alleyway as they were making their way down the street.

"I told you to come alone," the man said.

Quinn stopped next to Mr. Larson and stood staring up at the huge man.

He stood well over six and a half feet tall and he was enormous. He was solidly built, all muscle. She tried in vain to see his face in the darkness, but under the fedora hat he was wearing, it seemed like shadow was always over his face.

"Did you do as you were told?" the man asked.

"Every bit of it," Larson said.

"Then why do you have an escort?" the man asked, nodding at Quinn.

Larson just sighed and looked at Quinn.

"She's nobody," Larson said. "She can go back and tell her boss she followed the wrong person, and that I really am dead."

The huge man shook his head no. "She knows," he said. "You failed."

"No, please," Larson begged. "I did everything you asked."

"You failed," the man said. "Unless she is willing to come with us."

Larson looked back at Quinn, "She'll come. She wants answers."

"You bet I want answers," Quinn said. "And I'm not leaving until I have them."

"You heard her," Larson said eagerly. "She said she'll come. Voluntarily."

The man just let out a chuckle and then turned on his heel and led them down another dark alleyway.

Quinn started wondering if this was a good idea.

It was too late to turn back, she thought. She was all in.

They reached a building that had a large set of double doors. It seemed out of place, from what Quinn could tell. She had no idea what would be waiting for her on the other side of those doors.

The man turned and looked at Quinn.

"You can't bring your phone," he said to her.

"What?" Quinn was really thinking this was all a very bad idea. She considered just turning back. Reporting what she had seen so far, and letting Mr. Nguyen decide what to do about the rest.

She knew Larson was alive.

But she still didn't know what he was up to, and that was part of her assignment.

Quinn looked around and then up at the man.

"What do you want me to do with it?" she asked.

He just put out a gloved hand.

Quinn pulled her cell phone from her pocket and held it in her hand for a moment.

Without her cell phone, she had no way to call for help. And the last time she had texted her assistant was back at the car.

No one would know where to find her.

She handed the man her phone.

He immediately dropped it on the ground and smashed it with one of his huge feet.

"Hey," she said. "Why did you have to do that?"

"No technology," he said.

She was suddenly glad she had left her purse in the car. Her extra laptop and personal phone were still safe in there.

"You can't just walk in here," the man said.

"What do you mean?" Quinn looked back and forth between the two men.

"Get ready for the ride of your life," Larson laughed. He hopped up and down and rubbed his hands together like a small child ready for a reward.

Quin would've thought he was crazy if her attention hadn't been drawn to the huge man standing in front of her. He bent forward and his arms grew long and changed shape. His body morphed in the darkness and he became a large black stallion, stamping at the ground in front of her.

"Now we ride!" Larson gleefully jumped up onto the horse's back.

He reached a hand down to Quinn. Still in shock, she absently reached up to Larson's hand that was extended down to her and he pulled her up. She allowed herself to be whisked up onto the horse so that she was sitting behind him on the horse's back.

"Hold on," Larson hollered.

The horse kicked open the double doors and Quinn was suddenly blinded by a bright light that appeared in the doorway. She involuntarily threw her arms around Mr. Larson's waist in a desperate attempt to not get bucked off and left behind.

The horse leapt straight into the light and the next thing Quinn knew, they were flying on horseback over a grassy terrain.

It was daylight and she could see clearly as they flew through the clouds and then angled down towards the ground at a frightening speed.

When they landed, she and Larson climbed off the horse together and stood looking around.

"Where are we?" she asked.

"Does it matter?" Larson asked. "Look at this place!"

Larson wandered off into the grassy field and behaved like he clearly saw something that Quinn did not.

The horse shifted again beside her and the familiar deep voice asked her, "What do you see?"

"Nothing," she shook her head. "Just Larson in an empty grass field."

She turned and looked at the man/horse, who was now a large rabbit looking down at her.

"What the heck?" she took a step backwards. "What are you?"

"I'm a pooka," he said proudly. "Look out at the field again."

"A what?" she asked.

"Look again," he pointed past her to the field.

When Quinn looked back, she was faced with the most beautiful garden she had ever seen. There was a tiered fountain in the center and the base was surrounded by beds of pansies.

A grass pathway went in a circle around it with pathways leading to large and beautiful beds of some of Quinn's favorite spring flowers. There was every color Quinn could imagine.

Sitting on the edge of the fountain was the most beautiful woman she had ever seen. She had long blonde hair that flowed down her back. She wore a green dress that was tied with a golden cord around her waist. She turned and saw Quinn looking at her, and she stood up from the edge of the fountain and started coming towards her.

"Welcome," the woman said. "My name is Aurora; you must be Quinn."

"How did you know my name?" Quinn asked.

As the woman got closer, Quinn noticed that the woman had pointed ears sticking out through her hair.

"I know the name of everyone who comes to my garden," Aurora said.

Quinn looked back at the pooka, but he was gone. So was Larson.

"Where did they go?" Quinn asked.

"Who?" Aurora asked.

Quinn looked back over her shoulder again. The garden continued on behind her, with its colorful flowers stretching as far as the eye could see. Butterflies flitted around everywhere, making the garden feel even more magical than it looked.

"I don't know," Quinn shook her head. "I thought-"

"I have something to show you," Aurora said.

She took Quinn by the hand and led her back to the fountain.

Quinn followed Aurora over to the water and looked into the fountain where Aurora was pointing.

She saw her own reflection in the water. She now wore a flower crown on her head and a golden dress that matched the one Aurora wore. Hers was tied with a green cord around the waist.

"What would you like to do today?" Aurora asked.

Quinn, completely unable to tear her eyes away from her own reflection, felt like she had come here for a reason. She just couldn't think of why.

"I don't know," Quinn said. "What would you like to do?"

Aurora smiled and said, "Follow me."

Aurora took Quinn by the hand and took off running. Quinn followed closely behind her, enjoying the feel of the warm breeze on her face as they went. They ran into a beautiful forest and Aurora showed Quinn the magic of the trees.

Quinn felt like she had never been so happy in all her life. She watched pixies playing in the forest and she and Aurora played hide and seek with them. She felt as if all of her worries and cares had melted off of her and she felt completely free.

As the sun was setting, Aurora led Quinn back to the fountain and there the pooka was waiting for her in his black stallion disguise.

"Come with me," he said.

"Where are we going?" Quinn asked.

"Climb on," he ordered.

"You'd better go," Aurora said. "But come back to see me soon, I had such fun today."

Aurora hugged Quinn goodbye and Quinn climbed up onto the horse's back.

The ride back was like a bucket of cold water being thrown on her and she remembered why she had come.

But by the time she remembered that she was supposed to be looking for what happened to Mr. Larson, the pooka was already standing with her on the dark street as the double doors slammed shut behind them.

"Wait," she said. "I need to go back."

Quinn threw herself against the doors, but they were locked up tight.

"If you're worried about Mr. Larson," the pooka said. "You no longer need to. He will never return to this world. You can tell your boss that you followed the wrong man and that Mr. Larson is dead and buried."

"I don't care about Mr. Larson," she said, pounding on the door desperately. "I just need to go back."

The pooka smiled.

"There are some conditions," he said.

"What are they?" she asked. She turned and looked at him with wild-eyed torment.

"You must sever all ties with this world," the pooka said. "You must rid yourself of all money, but you cannot spend it nor can you give it away to someone who needs it or will use it."

"What?" she asked. "Why?"

"These are the conditions," he said. "You must fake your death. No one must come looking for you. That is where Mr. Larson failed us."

"What happens if I fail?" she asked.

"Then you cannot enter back into our world," he said.

"But you let Larson back in," she said.

The pooka just laughed. "Did we?"

"Didn't you?" she asked.

"And finally," the pooka stared down at her. "You will never return to this world. You will stay with us forever."

"Okay," she said. "Fine, whatever."

"You may return to us when these things are done," the pooka said.

"Okay," she said. "I'll be back."

Quinn ran to her car.

She breathlessly texted her assistant that it was the wrong man, and that she was on her way home.

The whole drive back to the city, Quinn had a heady feeling that made everything feel like a dream. She couldn't stop thinking about Aurora's world and getting back to it. She longed for the feeling of freedom and happiness that she experienced while she was there.

When she got home, she set out to create a trust to take care of her money and other assets. She set it up the same way Mr. Larson had, leaving the money to a large business with the recommendation that they give it all to charity on their own behalf.

Then she set out to fake her own death.

In her hurry, she decided that the best way was to push her car into the river. Hopefully the authorities would find it, and assume she had drowned, and declare her dead after she had been missing for a while.

She then bought a bus ticket with a small stash of cash she had set aside for the trip, and headed back to New Orleans.

It was a long bus ride. When she finally got there, she waited for the pooka in front of the double doors, anxious to get back to the garden.

Late that night, he finally showed up.

"You had a lot of people looking for you," he said.

"What?" she didn't understand.

"You failed the test when you had people searching for your body," he said. "People are still looking for you."

"But they will declare me dead soon and no one will ever find me anyway," Quinn said desperately. "Just take me back."

The pooka smiled and opened the doors. He turned into the black stallion so she could climb up onto his back and they flew back to the grassy field.

Quinn climbed off of the horse's back and ran towards the tiered fountain to wait for her friend. She called out to Aurora.

But no one came.

The only soul she saw was Mr. Larson. He was wandering around calling for someone, but Quinn couldn't make out the name.

"Mr. Larson," she called out to him.

"Quinn, are you back?" he came over and seemed confused to see her.

"I guess," she said. "But I don't see Aurora anywhere."

"I haven't seen my friend Reggie in years," he said.

"Years?" Quinn asked.

"Yes, I have been coming back here every day for three years now, but you're the first person I have seen in that entire time," he said. "How long did it take you to get back here?"

"I was gone for about three weeks," Quinn said. "I had to set up my trust."

"Three weeks?" Larson asked. "Tell me, did the pooka say that you failed at any of the conditions?"

"Yes," Quinn admitted. "I failed at faking my death. They had to search for my body."

Larson shook his head. "You should have taken longer to plan," he said.

"Why?" Quinn asked.

"I think this is the punishment for failing," he said sadly.

"What is?" she asked.

"We're trapped here, forever," he said. "Without getting to see the friend we made. Without getting to see the magical forest again. We're just trapped."

"That can't be right," Quinn said. "They wouldn't just leave us here. Aurora wouldn't just leave me here."

"But they did," Larson said.

"But why?" she asked. "To what end?"

"I don't know," Larson said sadly. "But there's no way home. Not that I've found anyway."

"So, we're just trapped here? Forever?" Quinn asked.

"I think so," Larson said. "There's no way home."

Quinn watched as Larson started to fade away.

"Larson? What's happening to you?' she asked.

But he couldn't hear her and he just disappeared.

Quinn started to panic. She didn't want to fade into nothingness like Larson did. She wondered if he was dead or if he would return.

She started towards what she thought the direction of the enchanted forest was and she walked for what felt like days.

When she thought she couldn't walk any farther, she saw the tiered fountain looming ahead of her. She had no idea how she had circled back to it.

She had no energy as she walked the rest of the way to the fountain. She felt completely drained of hope.

When she finally got back to the fountain, Aurora appeared and sat down next to her.

"What is happening?" Quinn asked Aurora.

"You weren't able to keep your end of the deal," Aurora said sadly. "So, we can't let you the rest of the way in."

"You mean, I'm just trapped here?" Quinn asked.

Aurora nodded sadly.

"Why did you come back?" Quinn asked.

"I wanted to see you," Aurora said. "It's against the rules, but I couldn't let you go on looking for me. You won't see me again. Not ever."

"Then why come see me at all?" Quinn asked.

"You seemed so nice," Aurora said. "I didn't want to watch you suffer."

"But leaving me here will make me suffer, don't you see?" Quinn said.

"No," Aurora shook her head. "You can end it quicker than that horrible Mr. Larson did."

"How?" Quinn asked.

"You must surrender to the despair and the sadness," Aurora said. "The creatures here feed on hope. They let you go when you don't have any more."

"What happens to me then?" Quinn asked.

"You just fade into nothing," Aurora said. "Just like Mr. Larson. Then you will finally be free of this place."

"So that's it?" Quinn asked. "Just give up?"

Aurora nodded.

Quinn broke down into tears, "I don't want to stay here. I want to go home."

"That's not an option anymore," Aurora took Quinn into her arms and whispered into her ear. "When you made your deal with the pooka, your fate was sealed."

Aurora wrapped her arms tightly around Quinn and started to sing a sad song. The music of her voice sent Quinn even deeper into despair.

Quinn cried into Aurora's shoulder until she faded away and disappeared.

Mona loved two things. Her garden and her horse. But when her parents separated and she and her mother moved to the city, she had to give up both. Mona was also faced with a choice. Should she meet her father's other family? She had a younger sister who wanted to meet her. Mona's choice leads to a new world that Mona never dreamed of, not even in her worst nightmares.

PlantMan662

* 1 *

Ramona looked out over the balcony and stared at the city beneath her. She missed the green grass of her old house. She had spent hundreds of hours tending to the garden that it used to overlook. There wasn't another building for miles. Just lush green and fragrant colorful flowers.

Here in the city, there was nothing but buildings. No gardens, no grass, very few trees. And the smell was anything but good.

She stared at her little balcony garden and watched the leaves of her tiny sprouts wavering in the breeze. She hoped that one day, her little garden would become a green wall, separating her from the horrific view of the city and give her a small sense of the peace she had in her lush garden before.

Mona loved two things. Her garden and her horse, Mia. It had broken her heart when her parents told her they were going to have to sell Mia because they wouldn't be able to afford the monthly cost of boarding her. They promised Mona she could do whatever she wanted with the money from the sale of her beloved horse.

Her mother had let her take over their apartment's tiny balcony. Mona got some long planters and various colorful clay pots that she had filled with seedlings and soil and put it out on the balcony. She also brought with her a few of the plants she thought she could uproot and bring with her in pots, so she didn't have to start from seeds. Her mother was working two jobs to maintain their tiny one-bedroom apartment, so she wouldn't have much time to use the balcony anyways.

Mona made the balcony into her one place that was truly hers. The one place where she might find sanctuary from this now horrible life. A life in the city, without her father, where her mother had to work day and night to support the two of them.

Mona was relegated to sleeping on the sofa in the living room, so her mother conceded the balcony to Mona easily, in hopes of repairing the damage moving to the city and losing the privacy of her own room had done to their relationship.

The balcony was tiny, but Mona considered it "her room." Mona sat in front of her planter boxes even though there was barely enough room to sit on the tiny balcony amongst all of the planters and pots.

Mona could smell the scent of the potting soil over the smell of the city. It brought a smile to her face, in spite of the view.

"Mona, come here, please," her mother called from the kitchen.

Reluctantly, Mona got up and went inside.

"I want you to make sure you do your homework tonight," her mother said, as she wiped down their tiny kitchen counter. "I put some dinner in the fridge for you, make sure you eat it."

Mona nodded as she watched her mother. It had only been six months since her father left, but Mona noticed that her mother looked ten years older. She didn't remember her mother looking so old back home in their old house. She had looked young and vibrant. But she hadn't had to hold down two jobs to pay the rent. She also hadn't had to raise Mona by herself at the time.

Mona hated her father for what he had done. The lies were the worst. When Mona and her mother found out that her father had a second family, it was devastating enough. When he told them that he was leaving them to go live with the second family, she wasn't sure her mother would ever recover. She wasn't sure that she would ever recover.

Her mother sighed and came over and leaned on the other side of the tiny breakfast bar that Mona was leaning on and staring blankly into the kitchen.

Mona knew what her mother was going to ask next.

"Have you made your decision yet?" she asked.

Mona shook her head no.

"Technically, she is your sister," her mother said. "If you want to meet her, I won't have a problem with it."

"Are you sure?" Mona asked.

"I'm positive," her mother said hesitantly. "We may not like what your father did, but that's not Silvia's fault."

"If I went to meet her," Mona asked. "Would you come with me?"

Mona stared into her mother's sad blue eyes for a few moments while her mother pondered the question. She could see the answer forming before her mother spoke.

"I don't know that I am ready for that step just yet," her mother finally answered.

"I don't know how ready I am either," Mona sighed.

"Just remember," her mother reached out and held Mona's hand. "None of this is your fault. None of this is Silvia's fault either. You two are the innocent parties in this. And if you two want to be friends, even sisters, that is fine. Healthy even. You two have a common trauma in this. You could help each other through all of this mess."

Mona nodded.

She hadn't thought about the fact that Silvia could be as mad at her father, their father, as she was. That there was the possibility that she and this stranger could bond over a common enemy. Their lying, cheating father. But there was also the possibility that this sister could choose her dad over Mona. That she would be happy to be the chosen daughter.

It was Silvia who had asked to meet Mona. Would she have asked to meet her sister if she had meant it to be a hostile meeting? Or was she just curious to meet her older sister?

Mona thought about the age difference. It was only three years. Her father had been cheating and lying for over 13 years. At least. That was most of her life. She felt betrayed that he had lied for that long. He had hidden this other life. He had done it so successfully. Mona and her mother never had a clue. His business trips seemed legitimate. It wasn't until recently that they found out that he never had to travel for his job.

"I'll be working late tonight," her mother's voice interrupted Mona's thoughts. "Make sure you go to bed at a reasonable hour. I love you."

Mona nodded as her mother grabbed her purse and ran over to kiss Mona on the temple.

"And remember to do your homework," her mother called over her shoulder as she ran out the front door.

Mona reached into her backpack, which she had left sitting on the counter when she went outside to the balcony to visit her plants after school. She unzipped the front pocket and pulled out the small pink envelope that she had been carrying with her for the last few days.

The perfect handwriting on the front intrigued her. It was so meticulous in a time where a lot of schools weren't teaching much cursive anymore. The letter inside had the same perfect script. Written on pink stationery with a purple pen was the letter that her little sister had written her. It was short and simple. She wanted to meet her big sister. Silvia was 12 years old and had always wanted a big sister. Mona, at 15, had been her dream come true. Despite what their father had done, could they please meet?

Mona had read the letter over and over again. She had to admit that she had always wanted a sister herself. She also had to admit that her curiosity was getting the better of her.

She decided she wanted to meet her little sister.

* 2 *

Mona hesitated at the front door. Her hand hovered in front of the blue apartment door with 137 in gold plated door numbers nailed to it, her fingers curled under to knock. But she couldn't bring herself to do it.

She had come all the way across town to meet her little sister, but now that she was here, she couldn't bring herself to knock.

Before she could change her mind, the door opened. Mona caught her breath as she saw her little sister for the first time.

She had golden blonde hair and eyes to match. Mona had never seen eyes that color before. They were striking. Her pale white skin made the golden eyes stand out all the more. It reminded Mona of a cat that once used to frequent her yard back at her old house.

"Hi," the girl said. "I'm Silvia. You must be Mona."

She smiled widely at Mona.

Mona was too shocked to react. She still had one hand raised in the air to knock on the now open door.

"Come in," Silvia grabbed Mona's hand and dragged her inside, and shut the door behind them.

The living room was ordinary. Mona didn't know why she was expecting something extravagant. Everything was in shades of red, which was her father's favorite color. Red walls, red sofa, red drapes, red pictures hung on the walls with red frames. Even the furniture was made from a dark red cherrywood. The reds were something her mother fought against, because too much red made her feel agitated and angry. Mona could feel the same thing, although she didn't know if it was the red, or the fact that she was standing in a living room that has belonged to her father for much longer than Mona had been away from their old house. This was their home. The other family. They had lived here for years.

"Come with me," Silvia pulled Mona away from all of the horrible shades of red. "I hate the living room."

Mona let herself be led down a small hallway and into Silvia's room.

It was a stark contrast to the angry reds of the living room.

The walls were painted a bright sunshine yellow and the furniture was all white. What caught Mona's attention was all of the plants. They were everywhere.

Mona wandered around the room looking at all of the plants. There were pansies and African violets sitting on the window sill. There were hanging plants of all kinds dangling from a bar that was mounted across the room in front of the window. The view of the city obscured by the wall of green that hung down with long arms to strangle the ugliness outside.

There were plants on every surface of the room. Small plants in pots sat on top of her dresser and on shelves of her bookcase. Mona ran her fingers along the delicate strands of English Ivy that trailed down one side of the bookcase, all the way to the floor. There were larger plants in big pots in the corners of the room, each plant in the perfect spot for how much light they tend to like.

"You like plants?" Silvia asked hopefully.

"I love them," Mona whispered. "I have a balcony that I am trying to fill."

"If you want any cuttings, you're welcome to them," Silvia said, standing uncomfortably close to Mona as she spoke.

Mona stepped back to look at her little sister. She hadn't expected to have anything in common with her sister but their father. She wasn't expecting this. The last thing she expected was to share a common love with her sister. Or to have something so bonding as sharing cuttings from her plants.

"I would like that," Mona said. She couldn't get over the yellow of her sister's eyes. It was creepy, almost alien. "You can have any cuttings from mine as well. Although I don't have a lot at this point."

"Did you bring any plants with you from your old house?" Silvia asked hopefully.

"Yes," Mona answered. "A few."

"Maybe I'd like a cutting from one of those," Silvia said. "Something that's been with you for a long time."

Mona nodded. She stared into the golden eyes that seemed to bore right through her and into her soul. "Sure, if you'd like."

Silvia broke eye contact and walked over to one of the plants by the huge bright window. "I'll give you a cutting of this one, it's my favorite."

Mona walked over to the window and looked at the plant. It was nothing like anything she had ever seen before.

"What is it?" she asked.

Silvia shrugged, "I don't know what it's called." She clipped a bit off the side, where the plant seemed to be growing wildly. "I love it though, see how it just seems to capture the light in its leaves?"

Mona stared at the clipping and stared in amazement as the veins in the leaves seemed to almost glow in the sunlight.

"It's a beautiful plant," Mona whispered.

"Take it," Silvia said. "It loves sunlight and lots of water."

"You don't know what it is?" Mona asked as she put her hand out for the clipping.

Silvia shook her head. "I can't find it in any of my plant books, or on any of my resources on the computer. It's a mystery." She shrugged as if it didn't matter.

"Maybe I'll have some luck looking it up," Mona said.

"Good luck," Silvia shrugged.

Mona stared at the cutting in the palm of her hand. She cradled it like it was the most precious thing in the world and stared at it as if it held her in a trance.

"You okay?" her little sister asked.

"Yeah," Mona looked up into the golden eyes of her sister. "Yeah, I'm fine."

"Do you want something to carry that home in?" her sister asked.

"No," Mona shook her head. "I'm going straight home. In fact, I should be going."

"Already?" Silvia whined. "But you just got here. I was going to make us a snack."

Mona shook her head, "No, thank you. I really have to go home and get some homework done. I just stopped by to meet you. That's all."

"You'll come back?" Silvia asked.

Mona nodded. "Yes, I'll come back. We have more in common than I thought we would."

Silvia smiled in relief. "You're welcome here any time."

"Thank you," Mona said.

"I'm going to love having a sister," Silvia said. "Are you sure you don't want me to make you something to eat before you go?"

"No, thanks," Mona said. "I promised my mom I wouldn't stay long for the first visit. I think this is a little hard on her."

"Oh yeah," Silvia looked at the floor. "I sort of forgot about that part."

"I didn't," Mona said.

Silvia looked hurt. She lifted her wide golden eyes towards Mona and they were filled with tears.

"You won't let that stop you from coming back, will you?" Silvia asked, with a slight quiver in her voice.

"No," Mona shook her head. "That won't stop me from coming back. You're my sister."

Silvia wiped her eyes in relief and smiled again. "Then maybe you'll come back again this week?"

"Sure," Mona nodded. "I'll be back in a few days. Maybe on the weekend."

Silvia seemed happy with the plans and showed Mona out.

Once outside the door, Mona looked closely at the plant cutting that sat in the palm of her hand as she waited for the elevator. There was no sunlight in the hallway, but the veins in the leaves still seemed to have a faint glow to them.

Mona squinted at the cutting and felt drawn to the little plant. She couldn't put her finger on why it was so intriguing. Maybe because neither girl could seem to identify it. Mona was anxious to get home and try to figure it out for herself so she could be the one to tell her little sister what the plant's name was.

* 3 *

Mona tended to the little cutting she had brought home with her immediately. She hoped the trip home hadn't made it so that the cutting would have a difficult time sprouting and taking root. She had a few small terra cotta pots left, so she filled it with moist soil and put the cutting into it.

She remembered what her sister said about it liking sunlight and water, so she made extra sure that the soil was thoroughly wet.

Mona then sat down at the laptop she and her mother shared and started looking up plants on her favorite websites. She scrolled through hundreds of pictures of plants and even studied hybrids.

After hours of looking, she still had found nothing on the cutting from her sister.

Mona took a few pictures with her phone and loaded them into a few plant forums, so see if anyone else could identify her plant. After feeling like she had done all she could do, she looked at the clock on her phone.

It was late. She still hadn't eaten dinner or gotten to her homework. Mona headed to the refrigerator and took out the dinner her mother had left her. She popped it into the microwave and looked at her homework while she waited.

She didn't have much. It was still very close to the beginning of the school year and so the teachers hadn't started piling on the assignments yet. The computer made a pinging noise from the website she was still logged into. She went over to check her messages for the forum.

There was one reply to the picture she had posted of her sister's cutting.

It read, "GET RID OF IT!" from PlantMan662.

The microwave beeped over her shoulder in the kitchen to signal it was finished.

Mona ignored it and started typing her response. "Why? Is it poisonous?"

Moments later, the response came back in a private message, "Much worse. Where did you get it?"

Mona ignored her dinner once again as she sat down and wrote back, "From my sister. What would be worse than poisonous?"

"Where did your sister get it?"

Mona continued the conversation with PlantMan662 and revealed that she had just met her sister that very day and that her sister had it growing in her bedroom and had given her the cutting because it was her favorite plant.

She asked again what could be worse than poison.

There was a long pause before he replied again.

"Did you notice anything strange about your sister?" PlantMan662 asked.

Mona paused before writing, "She has yellow eyes. Like a cat."

"Don't go back to see her. Throw away the cutting. Down the garbage disposal," PlantMan662 responded.

"Why?" Mona typed back.

After another long pause, which seemed like forever to Mona, PlantMan662 answered back, "She's fae. Probably a changeling. She wants to kidnap you."

"She's what???" Mona replied.

PlantMan662 had logged off.

4

Mona spent the rest of the evening on the internet. She looked up everything she could about fae and changelings. She sat at the kitchen counter with the laptop glowing in the darkness, her dinner still uneaten in the microwave.

Her mother came home from work well after midnight, and she found Mona still deep in research on the computer.

"What are you doing?" her mother asked.

Mona quickly closed the laptop. "I was just doing some research."

Mona's mother opened the microwave that was blinking END in the dark kitchen. "You didn't eat your dinner."

"I must've forgot," Mona muttered. "I was just really into my homework."

"Well, did you at least finish that?" her mother asked as she pulled the plate out of the microwave and gave the cold food a poke with her index finger.

"Mostly," Mona said. "There's still some research I'd like to get done."

"What class?" her mother asked, trashing the food on the plate.

"Uh, science," Mona lied.

"Well, will you at least eat a bowl of cereal and go to bed within an hour?" her mother asked.

"Yeah," Mona nodded. "I promise."

"Ok," her mother kissed Mona's forehead as she walked past her towards her room. "I'm beat. I have to get up early. So, I'm going to bed. Make sure you're not far behind me."

"Ok, I promise," Mona said. "Good night."

"Good night," her mother said as she shut her bedroom door.

Mona stared into the darkness where her mother had disappeared into her room. She hated that her mother had to work so many hours. She hated that they had to live in the city, instead of their nice home on a big piece of property. She knew her mother hated it as well, but that she did what she had to do.

Mona couldn't let anything else bad happen to her family.

She opened the computer again and stared at the website she had been reading.

It described different legends about changelings.

Mona found the whole idea of fae being real to be ridiculous. But the more she read about the different legends from around the world and how similar some of them seemed, the more she thought that there could be the possibility of them being real.

She shook her head and thought she was being crazy from being overtired and decided it was time to get some sleep.

Mona walked over to the couch and laid down. She had forgotten to eat some cereal, and her homework remained undone.

Mona's mind reeled with the images from the internet and she fell asleep dreaming about changelings and fae.

* 5 *

Mona woke up the next morning to find that her mother had already left for work.

She stumbled off of the couch and untangled herself from the purple and blue crocheted afghan her mother must have put over her before she left for her day job.

Mona staggered to the kitchen, rubbing the sleep from her eyes. She found a pot of hot coffee and a note from her mother stuck to the coffee maker.

It simply said, "EAT BREAKFAST!"

Mona reached up into the cabinet above the coffee maker and pulled down a mug and a bowl.

She first filled the mug with coffee and added cream and sugar to it. She inhaled the welcoming scent of the first coffee of the morning and took a sip. She then grabbed a box of cereal out of the pantry and put some in a bowl. After adding some milk, she grabbed a spoon and started to eat.

She hadn't realized how hungry she was until she had started eating. She wound up pouring more cereal into the milk that was left in the bottom of the bowl and ate her second helping just as fast as the first.

She put her bowl in the sink and grabbed her coffee and headed out onto her little balcony.

The sun was already up and was peeking out at her from between the buildings that blocked her view of the sky. Mona sighed and sat down in front of her planter boxes. She looked over at the cutting from Silvia and almost dropped her mug.

The single cutting had tripled in size overnight. It was no longer the tiny little cutting that it was the day before. It was now a lush healthy small plant. Mona reached for it and pulled it gently away from the soil. Instead of popping right out like a new cutting would, a solid root system held the plant in place in the pot. Mona used her fingers to clear away some of the dirt to make sure. There was a full root system already established in the pot.

Mona let go of the plant and immediately went inside and washed her hands. She still didn't know what kind of plant it was, and she didn't know what it might do to her. PlantMan662 didn't seem so crazy to her anymore.

Mona went over to her computer and logged back into the forum where she had met PlantMan662. She typed in a private message telling him about the plant's growth and then waited.

She continued researching plants and fae until, a few hours later, PlantMan662 responded to her message.

"I told you to put it down the garbage disposal," PlantMan662 replied. "Now it might be too late."

"Why would it be too late?" she asked.

"Because now it has roots," PlantMan662 responded. "It's more difficult to destroy if it has roots."

"What do I do with it?" she asked.

"Do you have a fireplace?" he asked.

"No," she replied.

"Find a place to burn it," he said. "Carefully. And watch the roots."

Mona logged off and went out to look at the plant once again. It was impossible for it to have grown as much as it had overnight. The plant seemed to glow more brightly in the rising sunlight.

Mona couldn't get her mind off of all of the information she had read on the web about fae and changelings. They were dangerous. They were not to be toyed with. They were not friends. Even if it happened to be her sister.

Mona thought for a moment. If her sister was a changeling, that meant that Silvia wasn't really her sister. Her sister was out there somewhere, kidnapped by fairies.

Mona shook her head again. How could she possibly believe in fairies? She was a teenager. She didn't believe in fairies any more.

She stared down at the plant in the pot and still couldn't get over how large it had become in less than 12 hours.

Mona went over to the couch and put on her shoes. She went out to the balcony and picked up the pot. She got some matches out of the kitchen and put them in her jeans pocket. Then she carried the pot down into the basement.

She had only been in the basement of the building once before. The super had showed it to her mother just before they moved in and told them that they could store extra belongings down there. He had locking cages to keep people's things separate and safe.

There was also a concrete floor and extra cleaning supplies stored down there. Mona remembered the smell of bleach and other cleaners and they burned her throat while she was down there. She vowed that none of her stuff would be stored there because she didn't want any of her belongings to smell like cleaning fluids.

Mona found a metal bucket that was with the cleaning supplies and some newspaper that had been tossed in a corner. As she walked to the door, she saw a bottle of lighter fluid up on a shelf and grabbed that too.

She took everything outside, back near the dumpsters in the alleyway behind the building and pulled the plant out of the pot. She put it into the bottom of the metal bucket and wadded up some newspapers and threw them in on top. She doused it with a little bit of the lighter fluid and then she took the book of matches out of her pocket.

It took her several tries to light the match and then it went out in the breeze that was blowing through the alley. She tried again, this time much closer to the newspaper wads and managed to light the newspapers on fire. The lighter fluid made the fire burst up quickly and Mona had to jump backwards to avoid the flames.

She watched as the newspapers burned down rapidly and the flames crept towards the plant at the bottom.

Suddenly, a shrill scream filled the air. Mona had to cover her ears with her hands. She dropped to her knees from the sound. Mona managed to look up and saw the plant trying to crawl out of the bucket. It was on fire and was using its roots as hands to try to climb out.

Mona staggered over to the lighter fluid and grabbed the yellow bottle. She aimed it at the plant and squirted more fluid at the plant.

The plant shrieked shrilly again and fell back into the bucket as the flames shot skyward.

The shrieking grew silent and Mona was able to stand up again. She stared into the bucket and looked at the plant. The fire was starting to burn down, and the plant's remains slightly resembled a tiny creature of some sort. Not a plant, but something more animal-like. The fire continued to burn it until it collapsed completely into ash at the bottom of the bucket. The fire extinguished itself and left Mona staring into a now empty bucket.

After Mona cleaned up any evidence of her having a tiny bonfire in the back alley, including returning the still warm bucket and the lighter fluid to the basement, she went back upstairs to her computer.

She sent a message to PlantMan662, "I did it. I burned it. It was a creature of some sort."

A few minutes later, PlantMan662 replied, "Good. Now don't go back to see your sister. Ever."

Mona sighed. How would she explain that? Not wanting to see her sister after instigating a visit and even taking a plant cutting? Suddenly not wanting anything to do with Silvia seemed awfully callous.

Mona wondered if those golden eyes really meant Silvia was a fae.

She decided she would go over to see Silvia one last time.

This time, she had a plan.

$$* 6 *$$

Mona spent the day researching on the internet. Halfway through the day, she realized that she had completely forgotten to go to school. After a few moments of panic, she decided that she would deal with the consequences when they came. For right now, she had more research to do.

Mona was now ready to believe that fae were real, and that her sister was a changeling. There was no other explanation for what she had witnessed when she burned the plant. Her sister was definitely fae. Mona had no idea what that meant for her father and his new soon-to-be wife.

When three o'clock rolled around, Mona was ready to make one more visit to see her sister.

She packed up a thermos she had filled with a special tea and a piece of wrought iron from a broken balcony rail she had found in the basement and put them in her backpack.

Mona took a deep breath and headed to see her sister.

Moments after she knocked on the front door, Silvia answered by swinging the door open with a happy squeal.

"You came back!" Silvia said happily as she embraced Mona.

Mona hugged her back, not wanting to give away the real intention of her visit.

Once inside the red living room again, Silvia offered Mona a snack.

"Sure, whatever," Mona agreed. Although she had no intention of eating or drinking anything her sister had to offer.

During her research, she had discovered that eating or drinking anything offered by a fae would make you theirs forever. Mona didn't plan to go that route.

Silvia came over with some cookies and milk and they sat down at a little table near a window in the kitchen.

The sunlight poured in through the window and made Silvia's golden hair and eyes glimmer in an eerie way.

Mona was becoming more and more sure that her sister was indeed, a changeling.

When Silvia went to pour Mona some milk, Mona stopped her.

"Actually, I brought some tea with me," Mona said. "I feel like I've been fighting off a cold. Do you happen to have a mug I could use?"

"Sure," Silvia went quickly to the kitchen and retrieved a red mug for Mona to use. "Here."

Mona took the mug from Silvia and pulled the thermos out of her backpack.

"It's my own special brew," Mona said. "Anytime I feel the slightest tickle of a cold, I make this. I never get sick."

She poured some of the tea into her mug.

Silvia leaned over the table and looked at the tea, "What's it taste like?"

"It's actually good," Mona said. "I put in licorice to make it taste sweet. And it's good for a sore throat."

"Can I taste it?" Silvia asked.

Mona smiled and slid the mug towards her sister. This was exactly what she was hoping for. "Sure, go ahead."

She watched as Silvia took a sip and made a face and shoved it back towards Mona, "Eew that's really gross. What else is in it?"

"Oh, some chamomile, ground up eggshells," Mona started.

"Ground up eggshells?" Silvia made another face. "Gross."

"It works," Mona said. She made a mmmm noise as she took a sip and tried not to make the same face that her sister did. "It's good.

"I'll stick with milk,'" Silvia said.

Just then, Silvia's mother came in the front door with their father.

"Hi, Dad," Mona said. The disappointment in her voice was more because her plan was now ruined, but she could see the hurt look on his face at the unenthusiastic greeting.

"Daddy!" Silvia squealed and ran into his arms for a big hug.

Silvia's mother came over and smiled at Mona.

"Hello, you must be Ramona," she said. "My name is Ella."

Mona nodded, "I know."

Ella sat down in Silvia's place across the table from Mona.

"I know a lot has happened, but I am hoping we can become friends," Ella said.

Mona shrugged. She was wondering if one sip was enough for the tea to work on Silvia, and if it was, how long such a small amount would last.

"What is this?" Ella gestured at the mug of tea. "It smells wonderful."

"Mona brought tea," Silvia skipped to the table, holding her father's hand and bringing him with her.

"May I try it?" Ella asked. "I just love licorice."

Mona shrugged.

Ella took a large sip and then slammed the mug down onto the table.

"How dare you come into this house with that?" Ella stood and leaned over the kitchen table and glared down at Mona.

"Ella, what?" Mona's father reached towards Ella.

Ella flipped the table across the small kitchen to clear the path between her and Mona.

"She put ground eggshells in the tea," Ella said.

Mona's father tried to step in front of Mona, who was frozen in place in her chair, "I don't understand."

"Move out of the way Micah," Ella shoved Mona's father to the floor with no effort. He slid into the refrigerator and bumped his head against it with a loud thud.

"Ground eggshells in tea make a changeling admit who she is," Ella said. "You thought it was Silvia? You were so wrong, child. The changeling is me."

"Run," Micah yelled from the kitchen floor. "Mona, run."

Mona scrambled away from the chair she was still sitting in and tried to make it across the red living room to the front door. She tripped over her open backpack and tried to get back to her feet.

Ella was right behind her and grabbed her by the hair.

Mona yelped in pain as the changeling started to change to her true form and pulled Mona by the hair to face her. Ella's mouth had grown in size and she had three rows of teeth. Her eyes were like a snake's and she had scales where her ears should be.

"Mom," Silvia was in tears. "What's happening?"

Mona managed to look over at Silvia, who looked honestly horrified at the sight of her mother.

"That's right," Ella hissed. "Silvia is only a half-breed. She's not the one you had to worry about."

Ella drew back her free hand, which now had elongated fingers and talon-like nails. As she went to swipe at Mona, she suddenly let out a hissing squeal and released her grip.

Mona dropped to the red shag carpet with a painful thud. She scrambled to get out of the way as Ella collapsed to the floor.

Mona's father was standing behind Ella, breathing heavily. The piece of wrought iron from Mona's backpack was sticking out of Ella's back. Her body steamed like it was cooking and then slowly disappeared.

"I'm so sorry, Mona," her father looked down at her. "She had me enthralled."

"What?" Mona looked around for Silvia.

The girl was slumped over on the floor, still near the kitchen table.

Mona crawled over to her sister, suddenly feeling sorry for her.

"What's happening?" Mona's father asked.

"When a mother changeling dies, so do all of her children," Mona whispered.

Silvia looked up at Mona with her golden eyes, "I really would've liked to have been your sister."

Mona's eyes welled with tears as she took hold of her little sister. As she did, the girl went up in a steaming billow, just like her mother. Mona was left with tears streaming down her face and empty arms.

Mona's father was already at her side. "She didn't know. She never knew."

"She didn't know she was half-fae?" Mona looked at her father.

For the first time in a long time, Mona felt like she actually recognized her father.

He shook his head, "No. She was a half-breed, so she had no real power. Ella never told her."

"Is Ella why you," Mona choked on her words.

Her father nodded, "I met her one day when I was out for a jog. She offered me some water. It was a hot day, and I was parched. And the water looked so refreshing."

"You drank something offered by a fairy," Mona said.

"I couldn't help it," her father said through tears of his own. "It just looked so good."

"It's okay," Mona whispered.

Mona hugged her father for the first time in almost a year. "Everything's okay."

When it comes to mermaids and finfolk, who can you trust? Della will find out the hard way.

The Sea Journal

The cold wind snapped at Della's face like a whip. She crossed her arms tighter across her chest, trying to block the wind chill from her torso. The incessant wind blew her long brown hair across her face. She didn't dare uncross her arms to move it. Her hair covered her eyes and mouth and got stuck in her eyelashes.

She jerked her head to move her hair, but the cold wind found its way down around her neck and to her shoulders. She hunched down again, bearing against the November wind.

The tourists were gone. She hid away as much as possible during the summer months, when hordes and hordes of vacationers invaded the town. Thousands of people crowded the narrow streets of her little beachside town. Locals didn't bother to drive in town during the summer. It took forever in the heavy tourist traffic to travel from one end of the tiny town to the other, down the main road of Hemlock Street. The population in the winter was under 2000, but in the summer tens of thousands of people visit for their beach vacation.

This afternoon, the beach was empty. The roar of the waves once again soothed Della's mind and heart, no matter how bitter cold. The smell of the salt in the air and faint scent of fish that always calmed her and made her feel like everything was safe and normal.

She came down to the beach every day. To stare at the grey water and the gnashing waves as they crashed and rolled their foamy white churn towards the sandy beach.

It was like a daily dose of medicine that she couldn't get in the summer months. She never went to the beach in the summer. It was too full of tourists and noise.

Haystack Rock towered in front of her. The puffins were nowhere in sight on a morning like this, gone for the winter.

A storm was coming, and Della savored the taste of the salt air before it hit.

She wandered closer to the monolith ahead of her. The tide was out and the tide pools were usually full of starfish, crabs, and other interesting sea creatures. She was wearing her blue and white polka dot rain boots to protect her feet from the wet and the cold. She stopped short because her boots didn't have the traction needed to explore some of the wet and slimy areas that housed the tide pools. She stood at the edge of the first one and peered over them with a cursory glance.

Farther in the rocky terrain, she could see something floating in one of the tide pools. It wasn't a natural thing. It definitely looked man-made.

She grumbled to herself as she sloshed her way
out over the slippery and jagged rocks and small
islands of sand and tried her best not to slip and fall
into the icy water in the tide pools. At one point, she
had to uncross her arms to keep her balance, exposing
herself to the bitter chill of the wind.

When she got to the object that was floating, she
saw that it was a small book floating at the top of a
pool, near the edge. It was easy enough for her to lean
over and snatch it out of the water. It was dripping
wet with the cold salt water and the pages looked like
they were stained with blues and greens.

She shook it off to get the excess water off of it
and then looked at it more closely. The pages were
blank.

It was a pretty book with faded blues and greens
staining the pages that looked like watercolors. She
decided to keep it and let it dry out and see what she
could do with it.

She figured it was better to reuse something than
to chuck it in the trash, and now it was one less thing
littering the beautiful tide pools on the beach.

Della headed home, holding the still dripping
book at her side as she walked. She felt slightly
warmer as she crossed Hemlock, out of the direct
blast of the November wind on the beach. The tall
trees towered over her to block the wind and help
keep her warm.

When she got home, she kicked off her boots and brought the little book inside and put it and her wet boots on the floor near the wood stove to dry. The woodstove stood on a tile area that was large enough to put things on that she needed to dry, as long as she kept an eye on them so that they didn't get too hot or catch fire. She placed the book so that it stood up on its pages, hoping that it would allow the pages to dry away from one another.

She savored the heat from the fire inside the stove and stood there for a few minutes, letting the chill dry out of her bones.

Della had left too much wood in the wood stove this morning, so the house was more than warm enough. She always had trouble gauging how much wood to put in when stoking the fire. She usually put in more than necessary, causing her to have to go upstairs to where the living area and kitchen was and open all of the windows to let some of the heat out.

Which is what she did.

Della tromped up the stairs in her red socks and took off her jacket and scarf as she went. She went to the front windows and threw them open, letting the heat from the house meet the cold air from outside.

She loved winter. Not just because the tourists were gone. But because this time of year, when the trees had lost their leaves, she had an ocean view on her second floor out her dining nook window.

In the summer, the view was blocked by lush green trees, only occasionally giving her a peak of the glistening ocean in the summer sun.

But in the winter, she could see the grey ocean under the cloudy skies daily through the skeletons of the naked trees.

She loved February best. Mostly because there were always two weeks in February that felt almost like summer. The sky was a gorgeous blue, the ocean sparkled in the sun like a carpet of diamonds, and the trees were still bare enough for her to see it from her window.

But November was good too. She loved the winter holidays in a small town. Even though she mostly stayed in and kept to herself.

She was still surprised about how much the people in town knew about her, even though she was an introvert who didn't go in for small talk much. She had only lived in town for a little over two years, but she was still considered an outsider by most of the people who were born and raised in the small town. But that didn't stop them from gossiping.

Della had moved into the house after her divorce. She had always wanted to have a place near the beach, so she used her half of the divorce settlement to buy a place of her own. A place that was finally near the ocean. It was situated two blocks west from the beach, and to make things even better, it was also two blocks east of a forest. Miles and miles of forest that she wandered through almost as often as she wandered down to the beach.

Della made a snack and sat down at her tiny little table in her dining nook and watched the ocean through her window. When she was finished, she decided to go back downstairs to see how the little book was doing.

She moved her polka-dot boots farther from the woodstove, as they were now bone dry.

But when she reached for the little book, it was still soaking wet.

Della frowned at the book and picked it up. It was still dripping with sea water and wasn't any drier than when she had set it down near the woodstove. There wasn't even a puddle on the floor where it sat.

The room was almost stiflingly hot. Della set the book back down on the floor and went over to the front windows and threw them open to let out more heat. She was sweating and felt like she was in an oven.

She looked over at her dry polka-dot boots and then back at the sopping wet book on the floor. She couldn't understand how the book could possibly be so wet in the dry heat of the woodstove.

She picked up the book again and felt the spine. She had hoped that it would prove dryer than the rest of the book since it was the highest point. Maybe the water had just been draining downward.

But the spine proved to be just as wet as the rest of the little book.

She flipped through the pages again, trying to decide if it was just a lost cause. But the pages were so pretty. The blues and greens were in soft hues and stained the pages in random patterns that looked like someone had hand colored each page with watercolors.

She set the book back down again and hoped it would dry out soon.

She went back upstairs and forgot about the little book as she went about her day.

***

The next morning, Della was out for her walk on the beach once again. When she got closer to the monolith that dominated the beach, she noticed a woman over by the tide pools. She looked like she was searching for something.

Della pulled her coat and scarf closer around herself and maintained her distance from the woman.

Della stood and let the cold wind and the salty smell of the ocean wake her up. She loved having cold mornings on the beach to wake her up more than she loved coffee, which was brewing at home as she stood in the sand. Her polka-dot boots did little to keep her feet warm, but they did keep her dry.

While Della was watching the waves, she didn't notice that the woman over at the tide pools had seen her and was heading her way. When the woman was close, Della finally tore her eyes away from the grey churning sea to the woman approaching her.

She was dressed totally inappropriately for being on the beach in the winter. She wore a seafoam green dress that seemed flimsy and summery. She wore no shoes and no jacket. Her long blonde hair reached almost down to her waist and whipped across her in the wind and flew out past her like a flag flapping in a storm.

"Aren't you cold?" Della asked when the woman got close enough.

"Did you see a book floating out in the tide pools?" the woman asked, ignoring Della's question.

The woman made no motion to indicate that she was cold. Her arms were down at her sides and she seemed indifferent to the frigid wind.

"Yesterday," Della nodded. "A blank journal."

"You have it?' the woman asked. She seemed suddenly very happy and anxious.

"Not with me," Della said. "It's at my house."

"It's very important that I get it back," the woman said.

"Sure," Della shrugged. "I can go get it for you. But it was blank."

"Blank?" the woman sounded surprised. "Oh yes, it was blank. But it's sentimental."

"Okay," Della said. "If you wait here, I'll be right back. Do you want me to bring you a jacket?"

The woman looked at her quizzically. "No," she shrugged. "But thank you."

"I'll just be a few minutes," Della turned and walked towards home.

***

The whole walk home, Della debated in her mind about the woman. Should she have asked her back to her house with her? Should she get her a jacket anyway? Why did the woman give her the creeps? And why had the woman seemed surprised when she mentioned that it was blank?

Della walked up her driveway and around to the side door that let her in near the woodstove. When she turned the corner, there was a man standing at her side door, trying to break in. He was wearing blue surfer shorts and a green t-shirt. He was barefoot and had very long dark hair.

Della stopped in horror as she tried to decide what to do. Part of her was urging her feet to run, but Della was so scared, she felt like she couldn't move.

"Hey!" she yelled.

The man suddenly stopped and turned to look at Della. His eyes were grey like the ocean and he had a long beard that reached almost to his belt.

Without a word, he rushed at Della and pushed past her to flee back down the driveway.

Della couldn't react quickly enough, and so the man slammed into her, shoving her to the ground.

Della felt a sharp pain in her arm as the man slammed into her. He had scratched her, right through her jacket, leaving a gash where the cloth was torn all the way to her skin and she could already see the blood starting to flow.

The man ran off towards the road as Della staggered to her feet. She covered the gash in her arm with her scarf and held it there while she tried to unlock her door.

Her hands were shaking, but she was finally able to get the key in the lock and open the door.

Once inside, she shut the door and locked it behind her and leaned against the closed door.

She stood in the hot doorway, just feet from the woodstove, trying to catch her breath. She glanced down at the little book that was still on the floor next to the woodstove. It still looked wet.

She tied her scarf around her arm and went over and picked up the little book.

It was still soaking wet. Which was impossible after spending the night just a few feet from the woodstove.

This time, as she flipped through the pages, she saw something different.

There were markings on the pages. On almost every page. She couldn't identify the language, but it definitely resembled writing.

Forgetting about the pain in her arm, and the man who tried to break into her house, she took the book and headed back to the beach to talk to the woman that she hoped would still be there when she returned.

Della walked quickly down the street, this time, the wind and the cold didn't seem to bother her. Even with a gaping hole in her jacket sleeve.

She reached the dune that she had to get over to reach the beach and she went quickly up it. When she reached the top, the place where she normally stopped to take in the view, she looked for the woman and headed straight towards her.

"I have it," Della said, holding it up.

The woman looked relieved.

Della walked towards the woman and stopped a few yards from her.

"Why didn't it dry out?" Della asked.

The woman looked at Della's arm with the scarf wrapped and tied around it.

"What happened to your arm?" the woman asked.

"There's words on the page now," Della said, flipping through the book. "They weren't there before."

The woman started looking around in a panic, "What happened to your arm?" she repeated.

"There was a man," Della said. "He was trying to break into my house."

"Did he scratch you?" the woman asked.

Della looked at her arm, "Yes. But I don't think it's too bad."

The woman walked up to Della.

"May I?" she pointed at the scarf.

"Uh, sure," Della said, not sure at all.

The woman unwrapped Della's scarf from around her arm and looked through the gash in the jacket at Della's wound.

She frowned and said, "You're going to die."

"What?" Della pulled her arm away from the woman.

"You were wounded by a finfolk," she said. "It is fatal to humans."

"What do you mean?" Della looked at her arm. "It's not that bad."

The woman shook her head, "It doesn't have to be."

"Why was he at my house?" Della demanded.

"Because you took my book home," she said. "He was trying to get it back."

"I thought it was yours," Della said.

"It is," the woman said. "But others would love to get their hands on my journal."

"This is your journal?" Della held it up to the woman.

She nodded.

"What language is it written in?" Della asked.

"It's an ancient finfolk language," she said. "My name is Nerissa, and my father is the King of the Finfolk."

"You're a princess?" Della asked.

Nerissa nodded again. "I'm so sorry you are going to die. It's my fault."

Della was about to object when the world started to seem like it was swirling around her. She fell to her knees and pitched forward onto her hands.

The sand was so close to her face that she could see the pebbles and cigarette butts that were buried in the sand. A tiny white seashell was next to her thumb. It was the sort of thing that under other circumstances, she would've picked up. But today, she was dying and she just stared at that sea shell as if it might be the answer to everything.

"Is there a cure?" Della gasped.

Nerissa paused for a moment before saying, "Yes."

"What is it?" Della asked.

"You become one of us," Narissa said. "But only few are chosen."

"I brought you your book back," Della said. "I could've lied and said I didn't have it. But I brought it back to you."

Della held up the journal to Narissa. "I brought it to you, no strings attached. Please help me."

Narissa hesitated, "I can't."

"Why not?" Della asked.

It was getting harder for Della to breathe. She started gasping for air.

"Please," Della begged.

Narissa knelt down beside Della, "You will have to kill the finfolk that did this to you."

Della looked up at Narissa. "What?"

"The finfolk that scratched you," she said. "You must kill him. Only then can you take his place."

"Why?" Della asked. "I can't kill someone."

"That is the way it is," Narissa said. "If I heal you, it will only be temporary. In order for it to be permanent, you must kill the one who poisoned you, and you take his place in the finfolk."

"I can't kill someone," Della said again.

"Then I can't save you," Narissa said.

Della could feel her heart beginning to slow.

"Please," Della said. "I'll do it. I'll do anything."

"Tell me," Narissa said. "What did he look like?"

Della described the man who was trying to break into her house.

Narissa stared at Della for a moment, with a look of shock on her face.

"That was my brother," Narissa said.

Della gasped horribly, with what felt like water filling her throat. She knew she was done. She knew that her life was about to end.

Narissa placed her hands on the wound on Della's arm. Della could feel the strength coming back to her. Her heart started to beat normally. The pain in her arm subsided.

Della stood up, her limbs still shaking horribly. She looked at Narissa.

Narissa no longer looked like the nice woman she had encountered on the beach. Her eyes flashed with what looked like lightning and she had no whites in her eyes.

"Why did you heal me?" Della asked.

"My brother is a traitor," Narissa said. "But I am forbidden to touch him, as he is forbidden to touch me."

"So, you want me to kill him?" Della said.

Narissa looked at Della. "Yes, you kill him or you die."

"What happens after I kill him?" Della asked.

"You become one of us," Narissa said. "You live in the sea. I'll show you everything. You will be my friend."

Della stood and looked out over the ocean and took a deep breath of the salt air. It calmed her nerves once again, as it always did.

She looked back at Narissa and said, "So how do you kill a finfolk?"

Keiko's mother stored an ugly brown jug on a high shelf and told Keiko to never touch it. It contained her most precious possessions, and they were not for little hands. But when Keiko gets old enough, she reaches for the jar, and her world comes crashing down around her.

Siren Bound

For as long as she could remember, there was a jar on the highest shelf of the kitchen. It wasn't a particularly pretty jar. In fact, it was downright ugly. It was a dark brown with red flowers sloppily painted on one side, and golden flowers embossed on the other side. The lid was made of cork and didn't fit correctly, so it was always set slightly askew in the top.

Keiko's mother had put it up there herself. She said that was where she kept her most precious possessions, so that little hands wouldn't touch or break them. She also gave Keiko a stern warning that she was to never, ever touch the jar.

Her mother never said much else about the jar or its contents. In fact, her mother was not one to say much at all. She was always very quiet and careful with her words. Not given to chatter, she spoke more with her actions than with her voice.

When Keiko was little, she always stared in awe at that jar. She always tried to picture what was in it. What was it that could be so precious that it would stay hidden away where no one could see, or touch, or enjoy it? Keiko never saw her mother add anything to it, or take anything out of it. It just sat quietly on the highest shelf, in all of its brown ugliness, hiding its secrets from Keiko.

One day, when Keiko was older, her parents were both at work and Keiko was home alone for the first time. She was finally old enough that her mother was willing to leave her home, alone, with no babysitter.

Keiko had been planning this day for years. It was finally the day that she was going to find out what was in the jar.

She pulled one of the wooden kitchen chairs away from the table in the nook by the window and carried it over to in front of the refrigerator. She climbed up onto the chair and reached as far as she could over the refrigerator and up past the cabinets, to the highest shelf where the jar had waited for her for what seemed like forever.

She could barely stretch her fingers up to the jar. She was just a little bit too short. Keiko climbed down off of the chair and grabbed some of her mother's cookbooks from a nearby shelf and set them on the seat of the chair.

Keiko then gently stepped up onto the chair and then, even more carefully, stepped up onto the stacked cookbooks. She reached for the jar once again, this time, she could just barely pull the jar towards the edge of the shelf.

The jar was sticky and covered with a thick layer of dust and grease, almost giving it a hairy appearance. It was slick in her fingers and as she pulled it a bit closer, it teetered on the edge of the shelf and fell forward. It bounced on the top of the refrigerator and then flipped down to the floor far below Keiko.

She looked down in time to watch the jar crash into the tiled kitchen floor.

She sound of the jar hitting the floor seemed loud enough to be heard by the neighbors. Brown pieces of shattered pottery skittered in all directions, sliding across the floor to all corners of the room.

Keiko jumped down from the stack of cookbooks on the chair and landed on the floor. As she tried to avoid the broken pieces of the jar, she lost her balance and fell sideways, using one hand to catch herself.

A sharp pain seared through her hand as a piece of the jagged pottery sliced through her flesh. A few drops of blood appeared on her palm and she drew her hand in sharply and grabbed it with her other hand to stop the bleeding.

She quickly and carefully stepped through the wreckage to grab a kitchen towel from the handle of the stove and wrapped it around her palm. She looked at the yellow fabric as it started to show red through the thin terry cloth.

Keiko looked down at the floor at the mess of brown pottery that had scattered everywhere.

There was nothing else on the floor.

The jar had been empty this whole time.

Keiko felt betrayed. For her lifetime, she had always wondered what was in the jar. She had fantasized about it being money or jewels. Maybe pictures of her mother's childhood, or letters from a lost love. She had pictured keepsakes from her mother's life before she came to America, or a journal from a long lost relative.

But never once had she imagined that the jar would be empty.

Keiko sadly went to the pantry closet to get a broom. Not only did she have to deal with the disappointment of the jar being empty, she had to face her mother and tell her she had broken it.

Keiko sniffled and tried to hold back the tears as she swept up the pieces of jar. She couldn't imagine what the look would be on her mother's face when she found out what happened. Keiko wondered if she would feel as betrayed as Keiko did by the fact that the jar was empty.

When all the pieces were in a pile, Keiko got the trash can from the corner of the kitchen. She pulled it over to the pile of broken pieces and squatted down on the floor to start transferring the larger pieces into the trash.

But when Keiko got a better look at the shattered remains of the jar, she realized that there was writing on the inside of the jar. She reached for more and more of the pieces and started trying to put the jar back together so that she could read what it said.

She ran quickly from the room and came back with a bottle of glue and sat down on the floor next to all of the shattered pieces of jar. She ignored the pain in her still bleeding palm and started to glue the jar back together, piece by piece.

She fit the larger pieces together as best she could and filled in the smaller pieces as she went. After what seemed like forever, Keiko finally had the jar pieced together in two halves, so that she could try to make out the writing on the inside.

The writing was faint. It had aged over time and was fading into the pores of the clay. As Keiko squinted at it, she realized that it wasn't in English, or any other language that she could recognize. It looked like tiny pictures, like hieroglyphics.

Keiko thought for a moment and remembered seeing a book in her father's study about Egyptians and hieroglyphics. She ran from the kitchen to the study and searched the bookshelves until she finally found the book that she was looking for. She grabbed it off the shelf and ran back to the kitchen and sat down next to the remains of the jar.

As Keiko started to find the different symbols in the book, she grabbed the pad and pen from the refrigerator where they wrote their shopping list and started to jot down the meanings of the different symbols.

Keiko spent the better part of the afternoon trying to decipher what was written on the inside of the jar. She lost track of time and when she was almost finished, she suddenly realized that it was time for her father to come home from work.

As Keiko read through the translation that she had been working on, she realized that she needed to hide everything. She quickly swept all of the tiny bits of pottery up and put them in the trash. She carefully wrapped the pieces of jar in a new trash bag and ran to her room where she hid the two pieces of the jar, as well as the book and her translation. She put the writing pad back up on the fridge and hoped that no one would notice the missing jar.

Luckily, when her father came home, he had brought home take-out burgers for dinner and he quickly took his and retreated to his study for the evening.

Keiko went back to her room and started to look at the book again, checking to see if what she was reading was correct.

When she heard the garage door for the second time, she knew it was her mother.

She waited to see if her mother noticed the jar missing from the kitchen.

Her mother didn't go to the kitchen. Instead, she went straight to Keiko's room and knocked on the door.

Keiko took a deep breath and opened the door to face her mother.

"Does your father know?" she whispered.

"What?" Keiko asked.

Keiko's mother pushed her way into Keiko's room and shut the door quietly behind her.

She turned to face Keiko and grabbed her by the shoulders, "Does your father know?"

"Know what?" Keiko asked.

"Does he know that the jar has been broken?" her mother asked. Her eyes were wide with panic and she was gripping Keiko's arms tightly.

"I don't think so," Keiko said. "How did you know?"

Her mother looked down and saw that book on the floor and Keiko's attempt at translating the symbols on the inside of the jar.

"That's my smart girl," her mother smiled.

She looked at Keiko's hand, which was still wrapped in the terry cloth towel that was partially soaked with blood.

"Did any of your blood get on the clay?" her mother asked.

"What?" Keiko was trying to make sense of what was happening. Her mother wasn't acting like herself.

"Did any of your blood get on the jar?" she asked again.

"I don't know," Keiko looked at her hand. "Probably?"

"You have to do something for me," her mother said.

"Like what?" Keiko asked.

Keiko's mother pulled her to the floor so that they were each sitting on the floor on either side of the broken pieces of clay.

"I don't know if this will work, but we have to try," Keiko's mother said.

"Mama, what is happening?" Keiko looked into the wide, scared eyes of her mother. She had always thought her mother's eyes were beautiful. They were a deep brown rimmed with gold, almost like a cat's eyes.

Keiko had always hated her own eyes because hers were the same deep brown, but only one eye had the rim of gold, making her look lopsided, rather than beautiful like her mother.

Keiko's mother unwrapped the towel from Keiko's hand and placed her daughter's hand on one half of the jar.

With the other half of the jar, Keiko's mother used a jagged piece from the sharp edges to cut her own palm and put her hand, palm down on the other half of the jar.

She grabbed Keiko's free hand with her other hand and stared at her daughter in the eyes.

"Now repeat after me," her mother said.

"What are we doing?' Keiko asked.

"Please," her mother begged in a whisper. "I promise I will explain, but you have to do this for me right now."

Keiko could see the desperation on her mother's face. She nodded and stared back at her mother.

"Repeat after me," her mother said. "The pronunciation will be difficult, but do the best you can."

Keiko nodded.

Her mother recited a few words that Keiko could barely decipher as words. She tried to repeat them as best as she could, stumbling over each word. Her mother coached her along, always in a whisper.

After several more sentences like that, she and her mother started to chant the same line over and over again. Keiko started to get comfortable with the sounds and was able to follow along without a problem after a few repetitions.

The jar between them started to glow with a golden light.

Keiko's mother's face lit up with happiness and she started to repeat the chant a little bit louder.

Keiko got louder as well as she watched the jar start to heal itself with the golden light.

She had never seen anything like it before and started to feel as excited as her mother looked as they both lifted their halves of the jar and pressed them together.

The golden light sealed the broken cracks and with a flash of blinding light, the jar sat between them looking brand new.

The flowers were visible again on the one side, but this time, they were golden and not red. They looked embossed and beautiful along the side of the jar. On the opposite side, where it used to be blank, there were smaller golden flowers that matched the flowers on the front with the exception of a single red petal on each flower.

"It worked," her mother said.

She was looking at the new, smaller flowers on the backside of the jar and smiled as she turned them towards Keiko so she could see.

Just then, the door slammed open so hard that it hit the wall and the knob stuck into the drywall, holding the door wide open.

Keiko's father was standing in the doorway looking angrier than Keiko had ever seen him.

"What have you done?" he yelled.

Keiko's father stepped forward and tried to grab the jar from Keiko's mother.

She pulled it from his grasp and handed it to Keiko.

"Stay back, and protect this," she said to Keiko over her shoulder. She then looked back at Keiko's father and started towards him.

Keiko held the jar close to her and backed up against the wall as far away from her father as she could get.

"Your spell is broken," her mother said.

"How?" her father asked.

"Your daughter," she looked back at Keiko. "Her human blood did it."

Keiko's father stared at Keiko, "What have you done?"

Keiko tried to speak, but the words wouldn't come.

"You've trapped her, haven't you?" her father asked.

"So to speak, yes," her mother said.

"Throw it on the ground, now," her father screamed at Keiko.

"No," Keiko's mother turned around on her suddenly. "Don't break it. Whatever you do, don't break it again."

"Keiko, you have to break the jar," her father said. "She is a siren. She is now bound to you and you to her."

Keiko tried to speak again, but still no words came.

Keiko's father looked to Keiko's mother. "You have to release her, she's your daughter."

"Yes, she is my daughter," her mother said. "And we are both free of you now."

"Break the jar," Keiko's dad commanded her.

"If you break the jar," Keiko's mother said without turning around, keeping her eyes fixed on Keiko's father. "We both die. Your father cast a spell to trap me. With the words that were written on the inside of that jar. He bound us together. If he died, I died. When you broke the jar, it set us free. And now you and I are bound. Mother and daughter. Free from the human that enslaved me."

"Why did you bind her?" Keiko's father asked. "Why did you drag your daughter into this?"

"Because I was hoping that you would value the life of your daughter more than your desire to kill me," Keiko's mother said.

"Keiko, listen to me," Keiko's father said. "If you break the jar, no one dies. It just breaks the spell. Your mother and I would both be dead if the jar breaking killed the ones bonded to it."

"Don't listen to him," Keiko's mother hissed and turned to look at Keiko. "If the jar gets broken, the magical being that is bonded to it only has a limited time to live unless the jar gets repaired. That includes you, half-breed."

Keiko clenched the jar to her chest tightly. She didn't know who to believe. She looked back and forth between her parents, the ones who have loved her and taken care of her for her entire life. She had never seen them seem unhappy, but now they looked ready to kill one another.

"I only bound your mother to keep her from killing others," Keiko's father explained.

"And the fool fell in love with me," Keiko's mother hissed.

"Please Keiko, break the jar, I promise nothing will happen to you," her father said.

"Don't," Keiko's mother said. "Don't you do it."

Keiko looked back and forth between her mother and father, and dropped the jar. It shattered at her feet and the sound of her mother screaming filled her ears.

Keiko's father leapt forward and grabbed Keiko's mother, he shoved her out of the room and pulled the door knob out of the drywall as he slammed the door shut.

"Help me," he said.

He and Keiko quickly pushed Keiko's dresser in front of the door.

Keiko's mother was screaming on the other side of the door, banging on it with all her strength.

"Quickly now," Keiko's father said. "We don't have much time."

Keiko stared at the door as it bumped against the dresser.

"Don't worry, she only has the strength of a human right now," he said.

Keiko's father gathered the pieces of the jar into a pile and sliced his palm with one of the jagged edges.

"You remember what to do?" he asked.

Keiko nodded, "But why?"

"Because now that you have been bonded, you will die without the jar," he said. "We must save the siren half of you. The bond keeps the siren from killing."

"But mama?" she whispered.

Keiko's father shook his head. "We can't save her now."

Keiko grabbed a piece of the jar with one hand and her father's hand with the other. She repeated the chant with him, over and over.

Soon, the golden light repaired the jug once more, the spell pulling the broken pieces together on its own. This time, the sloppy red flowers were on the front again with the small golden flowers each with a red petal on the back.

On the other side of the door, Keiko's mother was quiet.

"Wait here," Keiko's father said.

He pulled the dresser out of the way and opened the door slightly.

He stepped out of the room and stooped down to where Keiko's mother was slumped down on the floor. He picked her up and pulled her into his arms.

"I really did love you," he whispered.

Keiko stood in the doorway and watched as her father cradled her mother in his arms until her mother faded away and disappeared.

Keiko's father wiped the tears from his eyes and looked at Keiko.

"You must protect that jar," he said to her. "It contains the most precious things in the world."

"What?" Keiko asked.

"Our lives," he said.

Blade's Yard

Blade watched through the iron fence as the girl with the black hair gutted the garden.

The garden had withered and died, just like the prior resident, and had left nothing in its place but rocks and weeds and the sickening scent of death and decay.

Blade was a grass fairy and she wanted nothing more than to have her garden back. She sat on the monument that marked a human grave and watched the girl from a safe distance.

The iron fence was always hard to get around, but Blade managed it, as did a few other fairies. It had been worth it when the old lady lived there. Her garden had been beautiful at one point. The type of garden that attracted fairies. But that was why she had put up the iron fence. She seemed to think that iron would keep the fairies out. She was wrong. Iron deterred some fairies, but it far from kept them out.

Blade sat in the sun, squinting against the light as the girl tore everything out of the yard.

The girl didn't seem to like the sun. She wore all black and was completely covered from head to toe, including a large hat that had a veil hanging down from it to cover the girl's pale white face.

She worked long and hard in the yard. She had already done the backyard. Which was why Blade was intrigued.

The girl in black had cleared the backyard completely and replanted the entire thing with herbs, spices, and vegetables. A true witch's garden. Most of the plants were medicinal in some way, and the girl had made sure to plant them while under the light of the full moon, giving the young plants and seeds strength from the moon's midnight power.

That was almost a month ago.

This time, the girl was working during the day. She had cleared the yard of all weeds and had gathered the rocks and placed them around the yard strategically. Then, she did something the fairy was surprised she could do. The girl walked the perimeter of the yard, tapping the iron fence as she went. She tapped each bar with her fingers as she walked.

An alarm went off on the girl's phone, she stopped walking and went to the device that was up on the porch in the shade of the house. She turned it off, dusted herself off, and went inside.

Blade flew down to the empty front yard and flew high over the iron fence and then all the way down to the freshly turned earth. The girl had dampened the effects of the iron.

Blade marveled at the fact that a human could have such an effect on the iron, but Blade was grateful to be allowed access to the yard so freely.

She looked around the empty landscape at the kingdom that was once hers, and wept tears of mourning for the dead plants that had been pulled out and left in a pile at the curb out in front of the gate.

The following morning, a truck appeared in front of the house. It hauled away the dead plants and left the desolation of the garden in its wake as it turned back down the gravel road and drove away.

Blade watched the front door with trepidation, wondering what the girl had in store for the fairy's empty kingdom.

Behind her, another truck pulled up. Blade hid up in the willow tree that hung over the eve of the house on the cemetery side.

She watched as the girl came out to greet the two men who got out of the truck. After a brief conversation, she opened the gate for them and the two men started to unload plants from the back of the truck.

It seemed to be a never-ending stream of plants that the men carried into the yard. Hope and happiness filled the heart of the little green fairy.

Blade was sitting so close to the edge of the branch that she almost fell off. Luckily, she could fly.

The girl helped the men by pointing out where she wanted the various plants placed and by moving some of them around to various positions as she watched the men closely as they worked.

They finished emptying the truck, the girl signed a piece of paper, and the men left her in the garden among a large quantity of plants that stood in black buckets and seedling trays.

The girl spent a large portion of the afternoon moving plants around and watching the sun as it passed by overhead.

She prepared the soil for the plants lovingly. But didn't plant a single thing during the light of the day.

She went inside in the late afternoon and Blade fell asleep in the tree as dusk fell on the yard.

In the middle of the night, Blade was awakened by the slam of the front door. She didn't know where the sound came from at first, but then she realized that the girl had turned on all the lights in the front of the house and was now outside. But the girl carefully left the garden so that it was solely lit by the light of the full moon.

The girl got busy planting all of her plants. Blade watched her from the rooftop of the old Victorian house. She was not as careful about hiding herself in the darkness.

She watched as the girl openly wove her magic into the plants as she placed them in the soil.

Blade gasped in recognition. She was surprised that she hadn't realized it before.

The girl was a mage. A green mage to be exact. And an extremely powerful one to be able to dampen the iron with the touch of her fingers. Blade sat on the edge of the roof with her knees tucked up to her chin and she watched as the girl wove her magic with the magic that shone down from the light of the moon.

Blade had missed the planting in the backyard. Now she was very sorry she had. If she had known that the girl was a mage, she would have watched through the night when she had planted the backyard.

Blade smiled to herself as she watched the show as the girl's magic floated up into the air and scented the night with her magical spice.

The girl stopped to take a break and get some water from a bottle that she kept on the front porch.

"You're up kind of late for a grass fairy," she said from under the porch roof.

Blade froze in place, not wanting to make a sound.

The girl stepped out from under the porch and looked up at the roof where Blade was sitting.

"Did you live here?" the girl asked. "In the old garden?"

Blade was hoping the girl didn't actually see her, as she sat carelessly out in the open. But of course the girl saw her, she was a powerful green mage. She was young, yes, but extremely powerful.

Green mages usually had the Sight and were able to see fairies without much of a problem. Blade kicked herself at not hiding herself better from such strong magical eyes.

"I can see you, you know," the girl said. "Don't worry. I mean you no harm. In fact, you can come down here and help if you'd like. That way you can make an area just for yourself in my garden."

Blade wondered what the catch was. With fairies, there was always a catch when making a deal.

"No catch," the girl said, as if reading Blade's mind. "I only ask that you use your fairy magic to make the garden strong."

Blade dared to move and she flitted down to where the girl could see her better. She sat on a pot on the porch and looked up at the girl.

"You mean I can have any spot I choose?" Blade asked.

"In the garden, yes," the girl clarified.

Blade looked around. "What are you going to be planting over there?"

Blade pointed to the corner of the yard, near the edge of the porch.

"Whatever you'd like, if that's where you would like to make your home," the girl said.

"Do you have any jasmine?" Blade asked. "I rather like jasmine."

"As a matter of fact, I have quite a few jasmine plants arriving tomorrow," the girl said. "If you don't mind going one more night without a home."

Blade looked up at the girl and smiled. "I think I will be busy working tonight, if you don't mind."

"Welcome to my garden," the girl said. "You can call me Libby."

"And you can call me Blade," Blade said.

"It is very nice to meet you Blade," the girl said.

"I think this is the beginning of a wonderful friendship," Blade said.

"I hope so," the girl smiled.

The girl and the fairy set about working together in the garden for the first of many joint ventures in that yard.

The Old Oak Tree

Samantha was out of breath when she finally stopped running. The tears had been streaming down her face, drying against her cheeks in the wind as she ran.

She had run until she was gasping for air. Her lungs felt like they were going to explode. She leaned against the old oak tree that was so familiar to her as a child. The rough bark was comforting, like an old friend. She pressed her back to the trunk of the tree and slid down to the ground, her shirt catching slightly here and there on the bark as she did so. She pressed her hands to her face and let the sobs rise from her chest and the tears flow like a spring waterfall in search of some sort of relief.

She hadn't meant to come here. She just knew she needed to be alone. To process the news for herself.

Her little sister had been sick of a long time. Most of her life. But she had been a fighter. Sam couldn't believe that the fight was finally over, and that her sister had lost.

Out of thin air, everyone started showing up at the house. Family, friends, neighbors. Her house was overflowing with people expressing their sympathy for her family's loss. And they were bringing food. An endless supply of baked hams, casseroles, deli platters, and desserts. Like food would make up for the fact that her sister was gone.

Samantha finally ran out of energy to maintain the sobbing and her crying reduced just to a steady trickle of salty tears and snot. She wiped her face with her sleeve, wishing she had brought a tissue. Or a whole box of tissues.

She looked around at her childhood hideaway. It was where she used to come when her sister wasn't doing well and the house was full of home nurses and IV machines.

Sam remembered the good times she had here. Back when she would make believe that she had fairies for friends. She would play in these hills with the fairies for hours, before going home as the sun set. No one missed her on those days.

The images of the fairies were so real in her memory. But she realized now, as a teenager, that none of it was real. It had all been the fantasies of a hurting child with a vivid imagination.

She sighed and rested her head against the tree. She shut her eyes and felt the tears continue as if they were in control.

Her hands drifted to her sides and she felt the prickly dry oak leaves beneath her hands. There was a sigh beside her and she felt something grasp her finger.

She looked down and saw Aurora, one of her fairy friends from childhood. She sat on the ground next to Sam, holding her finger.

"You're real?" Sam gasped.

The fairy smiled up at her. "Whenever you need me to be."

Moth to the Flame

Nixie watched intently as the human boy walked towards the fairy circle.

Humans were suckers for fairy circles. Nixie knew that to capture a human, all she had to do was lay out some colorful mushrooms in a circle underneath a tree and human children were drawn to it like a moth to a flame.

Nixie usually just toyed with humans when she caught them. Just like any other fairy. But this time was different.

Nixie was tired of being different herself, and this human was going to change things for her.

He was going to change everything.

No longer would Nixie be the outcast of the fairies. She would be able to join in with the other fae after this day.

The boy was young, maybe nine or ten in human years. His brown hair tumbled over his eyes in errant curls that he flipped aside with a twitch of his head.

He stared down at the circle of mushrooms and then looked around him. His eyes were searching for fairies. She could tell he was looking for something hidden. He was looking for her, although he didn't quite know it yet.

Nixie looked around her as well too. She saw a bird above her. Its beak was open and its chest was vibrating as it sang its song out into the forest. A song that Nixie herself had never heard. But she knew it was beautiful. And she longed to hear it for herself.

Nixie watched the leaves blow in the breeze. She knew that the leaves sang a tune as well. Yet another thing she had never heard. But she knew the other fairies could hear it.

It had taken her a long time to figure out that the other fairies could hear things she could not. It wasn't something that had registered to her because it was something she had never experienced.

The other fairies knew she was different and they bullied her in merciless ways. Nixie shuddered as she tried to block all of the horribleness out of her mind.

It had taken her many years, and many failures, but this time she knew she had the magic right.

All she had to do was wait for the human boy to step into the fairy ring and she would be able to steal his hearing away from him. And then she would be just like all the other fairies.

She watched with tingling anticipation as the boy drew closer to the fairy ring. Just before he stepped over the mushrooms and entered the circle, Nixie felt a slight pang of guilt as she thought about what she was about to do to this human boy. To his life.

But more than anything, Nixie wanted to belong. She wanted to hear, so she could be like the other fairies. So the bullying would stop and so she would finally know what it meant to belong. What it meant to have a friend.

The boy stepped into the fairy ring and sat down on the ground in the center, just like all of the other children who came to this forest searching for fairies.

Nixie pushed aside all of her guilt and rushed forward towards the boy. She cast her spell on him before he ever even saw her.

She tore the hearing right from his ears and she quickly gobbled down the magic and waited for the glorious sounds she had been expecting to wash over her.

But they didn't. She remained engulfed in a world of silence.

The boy's face brightened as he saw her.

He made some gestures with his hands and looked at her expectantly.

She shook her head at him and shrugged.

He smiled and laughed and waved hello.

She weakly waved back, still trying to understand where her spell went wrong.

The boy waved her over to him and made a few more gestures with his hands.

She slowly, carefully approached him.

Nixie had gotten good at reading lips over the years and she watched carefully as the boy used his hands while he spoke.

"I'm Oliver," she watched his mouth form the words. "Are you deaf too?"

Nixie blinked in surprise as the boy smiled at her and made more gestures in the air. She watched and realized that he was trying to speak to her with his hands.

Nixie laughed in relief as she saw the human in the circle in a whole new way.

Olivia and her new stepdad can't communicate. Separated by language and cultural barriers, it takes a neighbor who knows ASL, a chihuahua named Chavo, and some motorcycles to help bring this new family together.

(And yes, you may be seeing a pattern with some of my stories. I am hard of hearing and have some experience with ASL. So sometimes I add some of that experience into my writing.)

My Fairy Godmother Wears Biker Boots

Olivia stepped off the smelly yellow school bus and breathed in the fresh spring air. That first step off the bus always smelled of freedom.

She slung her blue backpack over one shoulder and zipped the bottom of her favorite pink sweatshirt.

She had some time before her stepdad expected her home, but she had nowhere to go.

Normally, she would've headed home with her best friend Emma. But Emma and her family had moved away.

Two days before, Olivia had hugged her best friend - her only friend in her neighborhood - goodbye. She and Emma had been best friends since the second grade. The last three years, they had been in every class together.

Olivia had watched as the movers packed the monstrous white truck full of all of Emma's family's possessions. She hugged Emma as they both cried buckets of tears, and then watched as the truck and Emma's father's SUV drove away. Olivia felt like a piece of her had gone with them and was now lost out in the ether somewhere between here and Emma's new home.

Olivia didn't want to go home until her mother got off work because the last thing she wanted was to be alone with her stepdad. Her mom had met him online a long time ago, but she had only met in person a few months ago. They got married shortly after that. Olivia didn't know him very well, so she wanted to wait until her mom was there, just to be a buffer between them. It was too awkward to be alone with him because they struggled with a language barrier. And it felt too much like a stranger was living in her house.

The dirty bus drove past her, growling and burping exhaust like a tired and worn out dragon. It headed down the street and turned the corner out of sight.

Since she had nowhere else to go, she decided to take a walk.

Olivia wandered down the streets of her neighborhood, kicking a small white rock that she had found along the way. Her brown ankle high boots had a squared toe that was perfect for kicking rocks.

Kick.

The rock spun off to the right, almost going into the street.

Kick.

The rock hit a crack in the sidewalk and bounced ahead of her.

Kick.

The rock skid straight down the street, hit the post of a mailbox, and bounced up and over the short white picket fence of the mailbox owner's house.

Olivia peered over the low fence and looked to see if the rock had landed in easy reach. It was a good kicking rock. She didn't want to lose it.

She could see the rock on the lawn, a few feet out from the fence.

Olivia looked at the house. It was well kept. The paint looked new, an off white with a dark green trim. The windows had dark screens over them, making it impossible to see inside.

She looked up and down the street. No one was out. She was completely alone.

Olivia took one last look at the windows and decided that maybe nobody was home, and if she was quick, she could grab her rock and be on her way.

She put one leg over the short fence and her brown boot sunk slightly into the soft, wet ground. There was a small garden that went all the way around the edge of the lawn. Her jeans were a bit too long, and the bottom of her pant legs got muddy in the soft dirt.

She swung her other leg over and traipsed through the wet dirt and rushed onto the lawn.

Just as she was about to pick up her rock, the front door of the house opened.

A small dog jettisoned out the door, yipping in a high-pitched bark the whole way. It was all white with ears that pointed straight out to the sides. She backed away from it as it limped quickly towards her.

"Don't worry," an old lady appeared in the doorway. "He won't bite."

Olivia looked from the tiny dog to the old woman. She had gray hair and round glasses that had very thick lenses. She wore a flowered sundress and big black biker boots.

"Sorry," was all Olivia could think of to say.

"Sorry for what, sweetie?" the old lady asked.

"For being on your lawn," Olivia said. "I just wanted to get my rock."

"Is that it there in front of you?"

Olivia looked at the rock at her feet. The little dog was sniffing it.

Olivia nodded.

The old lady came down the walkway and out onto the lawn. She picked up the rock and looked it over, turning it over and over in her old wrinkled hands.

"That's a nice one," the old lady said. "I would've gone after it myself."

Olivia didn't know what to say, so she stayed quiet.

"Here you go," the old lady held it out to Olivia. "Finders keepers."

Olivia put her hand out and took the rock from the old lady.

"Thank you," Olivia said.

"What's your name?" the old lady asked.

"Olivia," Olivia said.

"Well, it's nice to meet you, Olivia," the old lady said. "I'm Flora Lefay. But you can just call me Flora."

Olivia nodded and looked down at the small dog that was now trying to sniff the rock that was in her hands.

"This is Chavo," Flora said. "He's part Chihuahua."

"What's the other part?" Olivia asked.

"It depends on the day," Flora said.

"Oh," Olivia was confused.

"Are you on your way home?" Flora asked.

"No," Olivia said. "Not really."

"Not really?" Flora asked. "Don't you live down on the next street?"

"Yeah," Olivia said. "But it's just my stepdad at home."

"Where's your mother?"

"At work," Olivia said. "I just don't want to go home when he's the only one there."

"Do you two not get along?" Flora asked.

Olivia shrugged and looked down at her pant legs, which were now soaking up water from the wet grass. "I just don't know him that well."

"Have you tried to get to know him?" Flora asked.

Olivia sighed, "I don't know. We just don't have anything to talk about."

Flora nodded.

"Well, since you aren't going home, would you like to help me with my garden?" Flora asked. "Somebody recently jumped over my fence and trampled a few of my new flowers."

Olivia looked back at where she had come over the short picket fence. There were two small plants that were squashed into the mud where she had stood as she climbed over.

"Oh!" Olivia exclaimed. "I am so sorry! I didn't realize-"

"It's quite all right, Olivia," Flora said. "I have a few more pansies up on the porch. We can just switch them out."

Olivia followed Flora up to the porch and helped her to gather up more baby pansy plants and the gardening tools that were in a bucket next to the plants.

Flora carried the plants while Olivia followed behind her with the bucket of tools. Chavo limped along behind them, yipping at butterflies and birds as he went.

"I don't have a set of gloves for you," Flora said as she pulled on a pair of light tan gardening gloves. "But there's not a lot to be done."

Flora knelt and pulled up the flattened pansies. Olivia watched sadly, feeling sorry for the squashed little flowers. The pansies that Flora had ready to plant looked a little bit like they each had a face with the hint of a smile. But the squashed ones had nothing to smile about anymore.

Olivia knelt down and helped Flora to plant the new little pansies. They planted the extras that Flora had left over at Olivia's urging, filling the sparse area a little bit more.

Flora chatted easily with Olivia, jumping from this topic to that. Olivia found herself wishing she could talk to people with such ease. She had always found talking to new people to be awkward and a perfect opportunity to embarrass herself.

When they were finished, Olivia helped Flora collect the trowels and other gardening supplies and carried the bucket back to the porch for Flora.

"Well," Flora said. "I think all that work on a warm day like this calls for some sweet tea. Would you like some?"

"Sure," Olivia said.

"Would you like to come in?" Flora asked. "Or would you be more comfortable out here?"

Olivia glanced nervously up and down the empty street. "Maybe I should stay out here."

"Okay," Flora said. "I'll be right back. Chavo can keep you company."

Flora went inside, leaving Olivia on the porch with the little white dog.

Olivia sat down on a front step and let Chavo sniff her. She put her hand out to the little dog and he stretched his nose towards her hand. After a few sniffs, he submitted to letting Olivia pet him. She ran her hand down his rough fur and started stroking his velvety ears. Chavo scooted a little closer to her so she could reach out and rub both of his ears at once. He moved a little closer and shut his eyes as she stroked his ears.

She laughed quietly while watching how content the dog was while he just stood in front of her and let her pet him.

Flora came out the front door holding two plastic glasses filled with ice and a brown liquid.

"I see you've found Chavo's weak spot," Flora chuckled. "Here's your tea."

Flora held out the blue plastic glass and Olivia took it. After a slight hesitation, she took a sip.

Flora sat down next to her and took a long drink out of her green cup.

"Aaahhhh," Flora said with satisfaction.

"It's good," Olivia said. "Thank you."

"There's nothing like a glass of sweet tea after working in the garden," Flora said.

"I've never had sweet tea before," Olivia said. She took another, larger sip.

"Oh, it's very popular in the south," Flora said.

"Is that where you're from?" Olivia asked.

"No," Flora said. "But I lived there for awhile. You haven't had real sweet tea until you've had it made by a real southerner. But this will do."

"How long did you live there?"

"Not long," Flora said. "I tend to move around a lot."

"Because of work?" Olivia asked.

"Because of work," Flora nodded.

"What do you do?" Olivia asked.

Suddenly, Chavo started barking and running with his limp towards the fence. Flora quickly got up and called to the dog. But Chavo continued to bark.

A lady was walking down the street with her dog. Olivia recognized the woman as her neighbor.

"Hello, Chavo. Hello Flora," she said.

"How are you Sam?" Flora asked.

"I'm doing good," she smiled. "I see you have some company."

Olivia stood up and walked to the fence. The two dogs were quietly sniffing each other between the wooden slats of the fence.

"Hi, Mrs. Natterstad," Olivia said.

"I didn't know you knew Miss Flora," Mrs. Natterstad said.

"We just made each other's acquaintance today," Flora said.

"Oh, how nice," Mrs. Natterstad said. "It's good to see you made a new friend." Then she said to Flora, "Her best friend moved away this last weekend."

Flora nodded and looked at Olivia. "Well, she's welcome here anytime. She helped me with my garden this afternoon."

"Oh, did she?" Mrs. Natterstad said.

Olivia hated it when adults talked about her when she was standing right there in front of them. She just ignored them and watched the two dogs.

"Well, I will leave you two to your gardening," Mrs. Natterstad said. "Have fun."

She and the dog continued down the street.

After Mrs. Natterstad was out of earshot, Olivia asked, "Why do adults do that?"

"Do what?" Flora asked as they went and sat back down on the porch step.

"Talk about kids like they aren't there, even when they are?"

"I don't know," Flora said. "I hadn't noticed that was what we were doing. I'm sorry, Olivia. I didn't mean to exclude you from the conversation."

"It's okay," Olivia shrugged. "I'm used to it, I guess."

"What makes you say that?"

Olivia sighed and looked into her now nearly empty tea glass. She watched the ice as she shook it back and forth to loosen the clumps of cubes. Like shaking dice in a Yahtzee cup.

"At home I'm left out of the conversation a lot," Olivia finally said.

"Oh, I'm sure your mom and dad don't mean to do that," Flora said.

"He's not my dad," Olivia snapped. "He's my stepdad."

"Do you and he get along?" Flora asked.

Olivia shrugged. "I don't know. He doesn't speak."

Flora paused a moment before asking, "You mean he doesn't speak to you?"

"No," Olivia said, dumping some ice into her mouth and chewing the ice before saying. "I mean he doesn't speak."

Flora thought a moment. Olivia watched a butterfly flit across the lawn and Chavo limped after it.

"Is he deaf?" Flora finally asked.

Olivia nodded.

"Aah," Flora said, as the pieces came together. "And these conversations you have been left out of, are in sign language?"

"Yep," Olivia said, chewing the ice in her mouth slowly.

"Have you bothered to try to learn sign language?" Flora asked with a smirk.

Olivia sat quietly for a moment. "No," she admitted. "But it's not like they are teaching me either."

"Would you like them to teach you?" Flora asked.

Olivia shrugged, "I guess."

"Okay," Flora said. "Here's what you do."

She gently pushed Olivia around so that they were facing each other on the front step.

"Do what I do," Flora said.

Flora proceeded to show Olivia a few signs, and had Olivia copy her hand gestures.

After repeating them several times, Olivia could do the without Flora's help.

"Perfect," Flora said. "Now when you go home today, sign that to your stepdad."

Olivia kept running through the signs. "What does it mean?"

Flora walked her slowly through the signs while saying out loud, "Please. Teach. Me. Sign Language."

Olivia repeated the signs a few more times while saying each word along with the signs.

"Cool," Olivia said. "Thanks."

"You'll have to come back and tell me how it goes," Flora said.

***

The next day, Olivia jumped down off the school bus and ran down the street, her backpack clunking against her back with every step.

When she got to Flora's house, the ran up the front walkway this time and up to the front door. She peered in through the front screen and called out to Flora.

Chavo came rushing to the door yipping happily.

"Come in, Olivia," Flora called from somewhere inside. "Just don't let Chavo out."

Olivia opened the front screen and stepped past Chavo. He stayed right at her feet, begging for attention. She bent down to rub his velvety ears before proceeding inside.

Olivia let her eyes adjust a little bit to the darker surroundings.

The curtains were drawn against the afternoon sun, making the room a bit dim. The front door opened into the living room. It was very neat with mismatched furniture. The couch was an antique style with a high back and tons of multicolored pillows. The arm chairs were overstuffed and comfy looking. Each side table had a crocheted doily made from a delicate tye-dyed yarn and had a Tiffany style lamp on it. Everything was mismatched and colorful, even cheerful, against the dim light of the closed curtains. Even the curtains were mismatched and colorful. The room made Olivia feel happy just standing in it.

Olivia followed a heavenly smell that led her around a corner, and she found herself standing in a bright and cheerful kitchen. The cupboards were painted in different colors and even the appliances were mismatched. Olivia's favorite was the turquoise refrigerator that stood stoutly in the corner.

"Hello," Flora said cheerfully. "Would you like some sweet tea?"

"Yes, please," Olivia said.

"Have a seat at the table and I'll bring you some," Flora said. "How was school today?"

"Fine," Olivia said as she dropped her backpack next to an orange chair and sat at the small green table in the corner of the kitchen.

Next to the table was a view of the backyard. Olivia was amazed at the wonderland of statues, flowers, fountains, and bird houses that were crowded into the small yard.

"And how did things go with your stepdad last night?" Flora asked.

"It actually went really well," Olivia said, her attention drawn back to the kitchen. "What's that smell?"

"It's zucchini bread," Flora said. "Would you like some?"

"Zucchini bread?" Olivia wrinkled her nose. "I don't think so."

"Oh, don't judge the bread by the vegetable," Flora came to the table with a small tray filled with glasses of tea and a dark golden loaf of bread that still had the slightest bit of steam wafting from it.

Flora sat down and handed Olivia a glass of tea and sliced into the bread with a long serrated knife.

"I grew the zucchini myself," Flora said. "Growing vegetables yourself makes them much tastier."

Flora placed a steaming slice of bread on a small plate and smothered it with butter and handed it to Olivia.

"Try it," Flora said. "If you don't like it, you don't have to finish it. But you can't not like it before you taste it."

Olivia took the plate and looked at the slice of bread. It had little flecks of green throughout, which Olivia assumed to be the zucchini. The butter was quickly melting into the bread and the whole thing smelled delicious.

She watched as Flora cut herself a slice and spread butter across her piece. Chavo sat at her feet, looking at Flora intensely, tail wagging, and drool leaking from his mouth down to the floor.

Flora took a bite and shut her eyes and said, "Mmmmmmmmmmm."

Flora took a small piece from her slice and fed it to Chavo, who swallowed it whole and anxiously waited for more.

Olivia looked at her own piece and sighed. She pulled her slice in half and took a small bite out of the middle.

It was sweet.

Much sweeter than Olivia was expecting.

It was good.

She took another, larger bite.

The hot butter made the bread melt in her mouth, and the sweetness was pleasant without being too sweet. She couldn't taste the zucchini at all.

"This is really good," Olivia said, taking another bite.

Flora smiled, "Thank you. I'm glad you like it."

Olivia gobbled down the rest of her slice and had another.

She washed it down with the sweet tea.

When they were done eating, Olivia sat back in her chair and looked out the window again. Birds and butterflies happily flitted around the yard.

"So," Flora broke the silence. "You still haven't told me how things went with your stepdad."

"Oh yeah," Olivia sat forward. "I did exactly what you told me to."

"And?" Flora asked.

"He started to teach me to sign!"

"I thought he might," Flora said.

"He taught me a whole bunch of signs. Like this," Olivia flashed a few signs at Flora.

"Very good," Flora smiled.

"Do you know what I said?" Olivia asked.

"You asked, 'what is the dog?' and 'who is the bathroom?'" Flora chuckled.

"Who is the bathroom?" Olivia asked.

"This is where," Flora signed. "This is who." Flora signed again.

"Oops," Olivia said. "I keep getting some of them mixed up."

"That's all right," Flora said. "You're trying. And you're doing well for only signing for 24 hours."

"How do you know sign language?" Olivia asked.

"My little brother is deaf," Flora said. "I learned sign language because of him."

"Was he born deaf?" Olivia asked.

"No, he got sick when he was very little," Flora said. "He lost his hearing and he and I learned sign language so we could speak to one another."

"What about your parents?"

"It was a different time then," Flora said. "They didn't understand that ASL was an actual language, so they never really learned it. But it helped my brother learn to lip read, and that was a useful skill for him in this world."

"Does that mean you could help me learn more signs?" Olivia asked hopefully.

"Yes, it does," Flora said. "I would be happy to help. And I'm sure your stepdad would love for you to learn it too."

"Oh, yes!" Olivia said. "He was really happy when I asked him to teach me."

"But you still didn't go home right away?" Flora asked.

Olivia shook her head. "He was going out job hunting today. He wasn't planning on being back until dinner."

"All right then," Flora said. "We'll go on to lesson two."

***

By the end of the week, Olivia had learned quite a bit of ASL. She was excited about finally getting to know her stepdad, and he was constantly teaching her at home.

Olivia was surprised how fast she could learn the language. Still far from fluent, and with a lot of help from his lip reading, she could at least converse with her stepdad rather well.

Each day, she stopped in to see Flora on her way home from school.

"How's your stepdad's job hunt going?" Flora asked at the kitchen table over sweet tea and biscuits.

"I call him Ryan now," Olivia said. "And not good."

"That's wonderful," Flora said. "Not the job-hunting part. But that you are calling him by his name."

"It's progress," Olivia smiled.

"What does he do?" Flora asked.

"He's a mechanic," Olivia said. "Mostly motorcycles, but he can fix cars too."

"And no one is very keen on having a deaf mechanic?"

"No," Olivia shook her head. "Which is stupid, because from what I can tell, he's good at it."

"What about his old boss?" Flora asked. "Is Ryan using him as a reference?"

Olivia shook her head, "No good. He and his dad ran a shop together. His old boss is his father."

"Which makes for a biased reference," Flora looked sad.

"He said the Deaf Community isn't strong out here," Olivia said. "Cuz we're kind of out in the boonies."

Flora nodded, "Yes, I've noticed that. He's a bit cut off out here."

"He's got a couple of old bikes in the garage that I think he is going to fix up and sell," Olivia shrugged. "He's been working on one of them on weekends."

Flora absently pet Chavo, who was in her lap fast asleep and snoring.

***

Olivia awoke the next morning to the sound of a motorcycle roaring its engine in the driveway. The engine sputtered and popped and then switched off. She looked out her window, which faced out to the street on the front of the house. She could see the driveway from her room.

Standing in front of the house next to a red motorcycle was Flora and Ryan signing to each other extremely expressively.

Olivia rubbed her eyes and looked again. Ryan was wearing his oil stained jeans and a fresh t-shirt. Flora was wearing an orange sundress and wearing her biker boots.

Olivia quickly got dressed and went outside.

"Hi," Olivia said.

"Oh, hello Olivia," Flora said, waving to her over Ryan's shoulder.

Ryan turned and waved at Olivia. He had a huge smile on his face. He started signing to Olivia excitedly.

"Wait," Olivia said. "Slow down." She tried to remember the sign for "slow down" which Flora signed to her behind Ryan.

Ryan signed much slower but was using signs that Olivia wasn't familiar with.

"I saw Ryan while I was out for my morning walk," Flora explained in English and sign language simultaneously. "So, I came over to say hello and we got to talking. He said he would look at my motorcycle, so I brought it over. It's been making a funny noise."

Olivia raised her eyebrow. "A funny noise?" She looked at Ryan.

He signed to watch.

Olivia watched as he climbed on and started the motorcycle. He put his hand on the gas tank. Every time the motorcycle made a rough chugging sound, Ryan pointed at the bike with his other hand.

"He can feel the noise?" Olivia asked.

Ryan smiled and signed, "Exactly!"

Ryan shut off the bike and went into the garage for some tools. Olivia watched as Ryan made a few adjustments and then he started the engine again.

This time it purred perfectly.

Ryan smiled, climbed off the bike, and gestured to Flora to try it out.

Flora got on the motorcycle and took off down the street. Olivia giggled as she watched the old lady ride off on the red motorcycle, whooping and cheering all the way down until she turned the corner.

Ryan looked at Olivia and laughed.

He put two fingers to his nose and brushed them downwards twice. "Funny."

Olivia turned at the sound of the motorcycle coming back towards them from the opposite side of the street. She and Ryan watched as Flora turned the corner and came roaring back towards them, her pearl necklace flapping behind her in the wind.

Flora pulled the motorcycle back up into the driveway and turned off the engine.

"Wonderful!" She exclaimed. "Thank you so much, Ryan."

Ryan signed that it was nothing.

"How much?" Flora asked and signed.

"No charge," Ryan signed. "You're Olivia's friend. You got her to start learning sign language. It's helped break the tension in the house."

"Let me at least make you some breakfast," Flora said, signing as she spoke. "Meet me at my house."

She started the motorcycle up and headed back towards her house.

"I guess we're getting breakfast," Ryan signed.

Olivia smiled and nodded. She helped Ryan clean up his tools and close the garage.

When they got back out front, Olivia led the way to Flora's house.

***

Ryan and Olivia walked up the walkway to Flora's house. Olivia watched as Ryan took in everything. The glorious array of flowers that seemed to be growing faster than possible and filling in the beds around the lush green lawn. He watched the birds darting through the garden and high up into the trees that arched overhead. The butterflies were flitting from flower to flower, dancing through the air with their colorful wings.

Chavo met them at the screen door, barking away and wagging his tail so hard that it was moving the entire back end of his body back and forth.

"Hi, Chavo," Olivia said as she opened the screen door. She bent over and scratched the dog behind the ears.

Ryan laughed when he finally got a good look at Chavo. The little dog ran around Ryan's feet and barked until he bent over and put his hand out to the dog. Chavo sniffed it carefully and then accepted some scratches behind the ears.

"Hi, Flora," Olivia called out. "We're here."

Olivia could smell the bacon as it sizzled in the kitchen.

"Come into the kitchen," Flora called back.

Olivia gestured to Ryan to follow her.

Ryan signed back, "follow your nose".

Olivia chuckled and went into the kitchen.

Flora had an amazing array of muffins, cinnamon rolls, coffee, tea, bacon, and other breakfast goodies already out and waiting for them.

"Who else is coming?" Olivia asked.

"Oh, a little much?" Flora laughed. "I didn't know what you two would like, so I got out everything."

Ryan took a long whiff of the cinnamon rolls and then signed he was hungry.

"Would you like some eggs too?" Flora asked.

"Oh no," Ryan signed. "This is plenty."

Flora served as an interpreter between Ryan and Olivia over breakfast. She let Olivia try her best at signing and deciphering what Ryan was signing but helped the conversation along by interpreting when necessary.

Ryan thanked Flora for encouraging Olivia to start learning sign language. He asked how she had learned.

"My younger brother got meningitis as a baby," Flora signed while she spoke. "He lost his hearing as a result. My parents were very old school and didn't understand the importance of him having his own language, so they encouraged him to read lips. But he and I found a teacher at my school who knew sign language and she taught us."

Ryan nodded and signed that he knew several people who had lost their hearing to meningitis.

He expounded and told them about each one, with Flora interpreting as he went.

Olivia was amazed at how fast he could sign and how quickly Flora could interpret.

"Wow," Olivia said when he was finished. "I've never seen him sign that fast."

Flora looked at Olivia, "What do you mean?"

"Well, my mom is still learning ASL," Olivia tried to sign as she spoke. "But they still have very slow conversations."

Ryan corrected some of her signing as she spoke.

"You married a woman who wasn't fluent in sign language?" Flora asked.

"Yes," Ryan signed. "We met online, and we fell in love. But my parents weren't happy because she isn't Deaf."

"Why would your parents not be happy about that?" Olivia asked.

Ryan started to sign too fast for Olivia to keep up. Flora interpreted.

"My whole family is Deaf. My parents, and their parents, and me and my brothers. We grew up in the Deaf Community. It is our whole life. Our family. And when I told my parents that I was in love with a hearing woman that I met online, they were very unhappy. They were even more unhappy when I told them I was moving away to be with her. It was a hard choice, but I love your mother very much and I was willing to leave my family, my community, my job, because I love her. She started learning ASL while we talked online. That way we could video chat with one another. But I am lonely because there isn't much of a Deaf Community out here. I have to drive to the city to meet up with new friends. But I need to find work so your mom can cut back on her hours. She works too much to support me. I need to work."

"If you can work from home for a little while," Flora interrupted. "I may be able to help you there."

"Really?" Ryan asked. "How?"

"I have some friends who ride motorcycles," Flora explained. "Motorcycles always need work. And not many of them can work on their bikes anymore."

"I can work in the driveway," Ryan signed.

"I will make some calls," Flora winked.

"Thank you," Ryan signed. "That would help a lot. Word of mouth is the best advertisement."

"Uhm," Olivia shyly spoke up. "What is the Deaf Community?"

"Deaf Culture is very important," Ryan signed while Flora interpreted. "Deaf people gather together because we have a shared language and a shared experience. When we are together, we get to be who we are. Not who hearing people tell us to be."

"What do you mean?" Olivia asked.

Flora interjected, "Hearing people see deafness as a disability, Deaf people don't."

"We can do anything hearing people can do," Ryan signed. "Except hear."

"But most hearing people treat Deaf people differently," Flora said.

"Like how I was afraid to talk to you?" Olivia said. She looked at her hands. "I'm sorry."

Ryan reached out to Olivia and lifted her chin, "It's okay." He signed. "You didn't know any better. It's hard enough to have a stranger in your house. But you had a stranger that you couldn't even communicate with."

"I could've tried harder," Olivia said. "Or at all."

"It's okay," Ryan signed. "We're past that now. I want to be your friend, okay?"

Olivia nodded and wiped away a tear that escaped down her cheek.

Ryan pulled Olivia into a hug that nearly off balanced her chair.

Flora just watched her two new friends and smiled.

***

The next morning, Olivia was awakened again by a motorcycle in front of the house.

She looked out the window and saw a man in a dark gray business suit waving his arms awkwardly as he tried to talk to Ryan. Ryan's face was concentrating very hard on the man's mouth. A black and red Harley Davidson was in the driveway. And an idling blue sedan was parked across the street with a lady behind the wheel.

Olivia pulled on her pink bathrobe and ran out through the garage to the driveway.

"Can I help?" Olivia asked as she approached the two men.

The man in the business suit looked at Olivia, "Can you tell him that I need my motorcycle fixed?"

Olivia looked at Ryan, who signed to her, "I got that. Who is he?"

"He wants to know who you are," Olivia said.

The man relaxed a little, "I'm a friend of Flora's. She told me to bring my bike here. But she didn't tell me he was deaf."

Olivia frowned a little, "But what's your name?"

"Oh, I'm sorry," the man put his hand out to Olivia. "I'm George."

"I'm Olivia," Olivia shook his hand. "And this is Ryan."

George awkwardly nodded at Ryan.

Olivia finger spelled George's name to Ryan, who then stuck his hand out and grabbed George's hand to shake it.

George was caught off guard by the handshake.

"How much does he charge?" George asked Olivia.

Olivia looked at Ryan, who had caught the question.

Ryan shrugged, and then typed something into his phone.

George read it and smiled.

"Great," George said. He gave Ryan the keys and his cell phone number. "I'll be back after work to pick it up."

Ryan took the keys and exchanged phone numbers with the man.

George ran across the street and climbed into the passenger side of the blue sedan.

Ryan and Olivia stood in the driveway and watched the car drive off down the street.

***

Morning after morning, Olivia got up early and helped Ryan with the people who showed up to have their motorcycles fixed. She got it down to a system where they filled out some paperwork that Olivia and Ryan had created to keep track of the motorcycles, keys, and billing.

Each afternoon, Olivia would first stop to see Flora, then go to help Ryan wrap up the day.

And each day, Olivia's sign language got better and better.

After a few weeks, when Olivia arrived home one day, Ryan saw her approaching and went into the garage. He returned and waited for her in the driveway. With a sad face, handed her a letter.

Olivia took the letter and read it. It was from the homeowner's association. Her mother was sent a warning letter about it being against the rules to run a business out of the garage. Olivia read it twice before handing it back to Ryan.

"What do we do?" she signed to Ryan.

He shrugged. His face was sad, and he looked defeated.

Olivia stared at the letter and tried to hold back her tears.

Ryan looked up and over Olivia's shoulder.

Olivia turned to look behind her, and when she did, she saw Flora walking down the street towards them. She was wearing a pink sundress with a huge floppy straw hat and her biker boots. She had Chavo in a little red wagon and he was laying on a purple pillow looking very regal and relaxed as she pulled him along behind her.

Flora waved and walked up the driveway, pulling the little Chavo wagon behind her.

Ryan greeted her and signed, "What's with the wagon?"

"Chavo needed some sun, but his arthritis is acting up," she said. "So, I decided to give him a little ride."

Olivia half chuckled, but then was serious again.

"Why the sad faces?" she asked.

Olivia handed her the letter.

Flora read it with a frown on her face.

"Well that's no good," Flora said. She handed the letter back to Olivia.

Flora thought for a moment. "We'll just have to find you a space to work."

"With what?" Ryan signed. "I'm not making enough to open a shop yet."

Flora frowned again, "We will have to come up with something else then."

With that, Flora turned the little Chavo wagon around and started back towards her house. She waved goodbye over her shoulder and Ryan and Olivia watched as she pulled Chavo down the street. The little dog looked content as he bounced over cracks in the sidewalk along the way.

Ryan looked at Olivia sadly and signed, "Let's go in and wait for your mom."

***

The following morning was Saturday and Olivia's mom had already left for work.

Ryan and Olivia were cleaning up the breakfast dishes when Olivia heard two motorcycles pull up in the driveway.

"Someone's here," she signed.

Ryan nodded and they both headed for the garage.

Olivia hit the button to open the garage door as Ryan walked through the garage to greet their visitor.

As the door went up, Olivia saw a beautiful new dark red Indian Chief Classic motorcycle in the driveway parked next to a red and black Harley that seemed familiar. The garage door opened to reveal two men standing there in jeans and leather jackets. One of the men's jacket was the same color as the Indian motorcycle. The men pulled their helmets off to reveal an older man with very gray hair and George, the same man that was Ryan's first customer. This time, there was no sedan idling across the street.

George walked up and shook Ryan's hand.

Ryan signed that the Indian was a beautiful bike.

Olivia walked up and stood next to Ryan as he admired the motorcycle.

"I have to tell you that you did a great job on my Harley," George said.

"Thank you," Ryan signed. "I love working on Harleys."

"This is my friend, Devon," George introduced them.

Ryan shook the man in the red leather jacket's hand.

"You seem pretty good with bikes," Devon said. "A few of my friends have been here over the last few weeks."

Ryan raised his eyebrows, "Really?"

"I have a shop a few miles from here," Devon said. "I need some good mechanics and I hear that you might be looking. You interested?"

"Without an interview?" Ryan signed.

"Your interview has already happened," Devon said. "My friends had nothing but rave reviews about you."

"It doesn't bother you that I'm Deaf?" Ryan signed.

"No," Devon signed slowly while he spoke. "I am learning ASL because my daughter was born deaf. You would be a great help to me in my shop, as well as helping me to learn how to communicate with my daughter. If that's all right with you."

Ryan smiled and signed, "That's fine. I would love to."

Olivia squealed and gave Ryan a big hug.

She was so excited that she couldn't contain herself. She signed to Ryan that she was going to go tell Flora the good news and she left Ryan to talk to the two men.

Olivia ran down the street as fast as her feet would carry her. When she got to Flora's house, Olivia slowed down and just stood and stared.

The front yard was overgrown with weeds and there were no flowers, no butterflies, and no birds. The house was rundown looking and it looked like no one had lived there in years. Olivia looked over where she and Flora had planted the pansies, and they were gone. Only weeds and dead bushes with layers of leaves and some stray garbage scattered about.

She walked up the front walkway, which had loose stones and was precarious to walk across. When Olivia got to the front door, the screen was old and rusty and hanging from one hinge. There was a note on the door from the HOA saying that the owner must bring the property back up to standards and that a large penalty was being applied to the homeowner's account that had been accumulating for months.

"Flora," Olivia called out. "Where are you?"

Olivia tried to knock on the door, but the rusty screen door wouldn't budge when she tried to move it. She knocked on the screen door and it made a metallic sound as it rattled in its single hinge.

"Flora?" Olivia called out again. "Chavo?"

Olivia heard footsteps behind her and turned to see Ryan coming up the front walk behind her. He looked as confused as she did.

"What happened here?" he signed.

Olivia shook her head in bewilderment, "I don't know."

Mrs. Natterstad was out for a walk and Olivia flagged her down.

"Olivia," Mrs. Natterstad frowned at her. "What are you doing there?"

"What happened here?" Olivia asked. "Do you know what happened to Flora?"

"Who, dear?" Mrs. Natterstad asked.

"Flora," Olivia said. "The lady who lived here."

Mrs. Natterstad shook her head, "No one has lived there in years."

"What?" Olivia said. "You saw us out here fixing her garden just a couple of weeks ago."

Mrs. Natterstad looked at Ryan, who was now standing behind Olivia.

She shook her head again, "No one has even set foot on this property in at least a year. The HOA is very upset about the state of the property."

"She was just here," Olivia insisted. "You even talked to her."

"Now listen here," Mrs. Natterstad was starting to get annoyed. "I don't know what kind of game you are playing, but the two of you need to get off this property and go home. I will be calling the police if you don't."

Mrs. Natterstad turned and left, with her bleached blonde ponytail bouncing behind her as she stalked off.

"We'd better go," Ryan signed to Olivia. "I don't want your mom to get another letter from the HOA."

"But what about Flora?" Olivia asked.

Ryan looked back at the dilapidated house. He shook his head, "I don't know. Maybe you can try calling her."

Ryan put his hand on Olivia's back and guided her back down the path and out to the sidewalk.

They both looked at the house one last time. Olivia could see a little red wagon in the bushes near the porch. It was overgrown with leaves and branches from a dead bush.

"Let's go home," Ryan signed.

Olivia nodded and the two headed back home.

"I got the job," Ryan signed to Olivia as they walked. "Pays pretty good too. Your mom can work fewer hours now. And I should be home around the time you get home from school."

"Great," Olivia signed. "When do you start?"

Ryan signed, "Monday."

Olivia looked back at the house one last time. A white bird sat up in the tree. It looked at her like it was satisfied and then flitted off down the street and out of sight.

*Short story telling the backstory of Shandoah, the dryad, one of my favorite characters from my **Fire Lily** series. This is a prequel to the trilogy. I hope you like the character as much as I do. She is sweet, spunky, and the best friend a main character could ever ask for.*

Shandoah

Shandoah ran through the forest, smacking the trees who were sleeping, just to wake them up. She giggled as she ran and savored the smells of spring as they were stirred up by her feet kicking up the moss and soil.

Shandoah loved spring. Most dryads did, although she couldn't understand how they possibly could if they were still asleep. In the spring, Shandoah couldn't contain her joy, hence the running and the giggling.

She could hear the angry shouts of the older dryad behind her, rousing from their hibernation. She ignored them and kept running.

Her bare feet slapped against the ground, intentionally splashing through the puddles left behind by a warm spring rain that she had enjoyed earlier that morning. Her toes squished in the cold mud and she loved the sound it made.

When she reached the clearing, she finally stopped. The sun was shining down through the gray clouds that were being blown away by the breeze. She took in the warmth and watched as the birds started to come out from their shelters to join her in the sunlight.

She spread her arms wide and soaked in spring. She relished the fact that the long winter was over and that, once again, sleep would be reserved only for night.

"Shandoah, come here," a loud voice said from behind her.

Shandoah cringed and she turned slowly to face the direction of the voice she knew all too well.

"Grandfather," she said sheepishly. Shandoah realized that in her haste, she must have slapped him as well.

"What is the meaning of your disturbance?" he demanded.

Her grandfather was standing in the clearing, also in his elven form. Shandoah could remember when they got along. When he spent more time playing with her and telling her stories while she sat on his knee, rather than lecturing her and yelling at her loud enough to scatter the birds back into the treetops.

"It's spring," Shandoah couldn't hide the glee from her voice.

"Yes, it is spring," her grandfather said, as he smoothed out his long gray beard. "But that is no excuse for your behavior."

"I'm so sorry," she looked down at her feet and noticed tiny little flowers were already peeking their way up through the grass. "I just couldn't contain myself."

"Well, try," her grandfather snapped. "You've awoken the whole tribe with your antics."

"Good," Shandoah said before she could bite her tongue.

She knew it was a mistake as soon as she said it.

"Good?" her grandfather took a step towards her. "You think your disgraceful behavior is acceptable?"

Shandoah felt a surge of bravery, or possibly stupidity, and said, "Yes! It's spring! Everyone should be awake."

Her grandfather took a breath to respond, but before he could, Shandoah let out a screech and then with a whooping yell and turned on her heel to run once again.

She hollered the whole way through the clearing and almost slipped in the mud as she splashed through another puddle that was a little deeper than she expected.

When she was sure that she had run far enough, she looked back through the maple and elm trees to make sure her grandfather hadn't followed her. She knew he wouldn't. He was too dignified to run. They all were, and that made her angry all of a sudden.

She looked around at the trees that were already showing their vividly green leaves. The sun was shining and it was a wonderfully warm morning. She couldn't understand how they could possibly still sleep.

She watched the birds cheerfully singing and flitting from branch to branch overhead. She caught sight of one of her favorites, a gorgeous robin, as it gathered materials from the ground. She watched in wonder as it flew up to where he and his mate were furiously building their nest.

"They're missing it," she whispered. "They're missing all of this."

"Of course they are," a tiny voice said from behind her.

Shandoah wasn't expecting a response. She whipped around to see a forest sprite hovering in the air nearby. The sprite was wearing the magenta petals of a fireweed as a dress. Shandoah could smell the petals from where she was standing, so the flowers were fresh.

"I love your new dress," Shandoah said to her.

The forest sprite touched the petals and giggled, "Thank you, I made it this morning."

"What's your name?" Shandoah asked.

"Sheyla," the forest sprite said. "What's yours?"

Shandoah," she answered.

"That's an interesting name," Shayla said.

"My mother is an interesting dryad," Shandoah said.

"Is that so?" Sheyla said. "I will have to meet her sometime. I like interesting creatures."

Shandoah was distracted by another robin, flitting around on the ground nearby.

"Where are the other dryads?" Shayla asked.

"They are still working on waking up from hibernation."

"Then why are you so awake?" Shayla asked.

Shandoah shrugged, "I seem to have more energy than most dryads."

"Oh lovely," Shayla said and she clapped her hands together with glee.

"What's lovely?" Shandoah asked.

"You're an interesting creature yourself," the sprite said.

"I don't know about that," Shandoah answered. "I seem to always be getting into trouble because of my energy."

Shayla smiled, "Exactly."

Shandoah shuffled her feet in the fresh dew on the grass at her feet.

"I was exploring the forest to see who else is awake," Shandoah said. "Would you like to join me?"

"Absolutely!" the sprite squealed. "I saw some of the most beautiful flowers over in a meadow, deeper in the forest. Would you like to see?"

"Yes," Shandoah said. "Lead the way."

The sprite turned and flew off ahead of Shandoah. She knew that sprites were creatures that were not to be trusted, but she was aching for adventure. She didn't see the harm in allowing a sprite to show her some early spring flowers in a meadow.

Shandoah followed her new friend. Sprites were surprisingly fast and Shandoah had to run as fast as she could to keep up.

The forest flashed by her in a blur as she kept her eyes fixed on the sprite and her little magenta dress as she darted through the trees. They went deeper and deeper into the forest, until they were in an area that even Shandoah was unfamiliar with.

When they reached the meadow, Shayla stopped so suddenly that Shandoah raced right past the sprite before she could will her feet to stop.

She skidded to a halt with a yelp and slid in the wet grass for another few feet before her motion finally ceased.

It was too late.

Shandoah slammed right into an ancient tree, rattling its branches almost as much as it rattled the teeth in her head.

The impact knocked the wind out of Shandoah. As she staggered backwards, gasping for air, she felt as if some of her magic had been knocked out of her as well.

"Are you all right?" Shayla asked.

"Stay quiet," Shandoah said. "Maybe it didn't wake him."

Shandoah's heart filled with dread and fear as she recognized the tree. It was one of the ancient ones. But worse than that, it was petrified.

Punished.

Imprisoned.

There was only one tree in the ancient forest that was petrified.

Anyon. He was a rogue of the ancients. He was petrified for crimes that were so old, Shandoah couldn't remember them. But she knew they had something to do with humans.

He hated them. Anyon wanted to eradicate them.

Dryads had no love for humans, but they didn't wish them harm either. They only wanted to live in peace, hidden away from human eyes.

But Anyon had tried to create dissent. He wanted a war. Shandoah racked her brain for what she had been taught about him. She remembered blood.

He had killed humans that wandered into the forest.

So, he had been petrified. His prison was hidden deep in the forest, where it was forbidden for dryads to tread.

Where Shandoah was forbidden to be.

This was a punishable offence.

"We have to leave," Shandoah whispered.

"No, wait," Shayla squealed. "You have to watch."

"Watch what?' Shandoah asked.

That's when Shandoah noticed the robin.

Her beloved favorite of the birds.

There was one at the base of Anyon. Dead. Its neck had been broken and cut, the bird's blood seeping into Anyon's roots. There was a circle of flowers from the meadow surrounding the base of the tree.

Shandoah looked at the sprite in horror.

"You're trying to wake him up," Shandoah said.

She spoke in a normal voice this time. Her whisper was lost somewhere in her shock and fear.

"I only needed one last ingredient," Shayla giggled. "The touch of a dryad."

Shandoah gasped.

She had been part of the spell. Shayla had lured her here on purpose.

"You used me," Shandoah said. "To wake him up?"

"We need him," Shayla said. "Don't you see? Too many humans have been encroaching into our forest. We need him."

"No," Shandoah said. "No, we don't."

Anyon's branches started to shake.

"I have to go," Shandoah turned and stumbled over her own feet trying to get out of the clearing.

"Wait," Shayla called out to her. "We still need you to finish the spell."

Shandoah was off and running again.

This time it was not fueled by the joy of spring. Her running was fueled by fear and horror. And the need to tell the others what she had done.

She would be punished. She knew this.

But her grandfather needed to know that Anyon was free.

Her grandfather would be the first one Anyon came after. He was the leader of the dryads, and would have to be done away with in order for Anyon to make any headway with leading the dryads to war.

She had to tell him. Now.

Shandoah ran as fast as her legs could carry her through the forest.

When she finally arrived back at her grove, a few more of the dryads had awakened. Some were still in their tree form, but many were in their elven form.

"Grandfather," Shandoah cried. "Grandfather, I need to speak with you."

Her grandfather turned and looked at her. His long gray beard swished in the breeze as he turned.

"Anyon," she said between breaths. "He's awake."

The other dryads gasped in horror. The forest went completely silent. All eyes were on Shandoah as she tried to catch her breath.

"What do you mean, he's awake?" her grandfather asked. "How?"

"A forest sprite, she cast a spell," Shandoah said. She was aware that all the dryads were listening to her now. But she didn't care. They had to know.

"She would need the touch of a dryad to wake him," her grandfather said.

Shandoah could feel all the eyes of the dryads on her now. She looked around and saw that most were now awake and she felt their eyes boring into her. She could feel their eyes as if they were tearing right through to her soul.

"She tricked me," was all Shandoah could manage.

Her grandfather sighed and looked at the ground.

Shandoah could hear the murmurs starting among the other dryads.

It was the first day of spring and Shandoah, the troublemaker, had already brought ruin upon them all.

"There's still another part of the spell that must be completed," her grandfather said.

"How do we know the sprite hasn't done it already?' Shandoah asked.

"Because you're still alive," her grandfather said.

Shandoah stared at her grandfather wide-eyed. "He has to kill me?"

Her grandfather nodded gravely. "Only the elders can break the spell without blood."

"So, what do we do now?" Shandoah asked.

"You must leave," her grandfather said.

"Leave?" Shandoah stared at her grandfather in disbelief. "For how long?"

"Forever," her grandfather said. "You have broken dryad law by releasing a petrified without permission."

"But I didn't mean to," Shandoah started.

"It doesn't matter," her grandfather said. "He is bound to the forest and cannot leave its boundaries until he takes your blood. You must leave, so that we may fix your blunder. But you are banished because you broke dryad law by releasing him, unintentional or not."

"But grandfather," Shandoah could feel the sting of tears in her eyes. "Where would I go?"

He shook his head sadly, "That is for you to decide."

Shandoah felt like the wind was knocked out of her again as her grandfather and the other dryads turned their backs on her and disappeared into the forest.

She was left, standing alone in the empty grove, with no other dryads except her mother.

Shandoah couldn't bring her eyes up to meet her mother's eyes. She couldn't stand to see the disappointment that she knew was there.

"My sweet child," her mother whispered.

Shandoah still couldn't meet her eyes, so her mother cupped Shandoah's chin and lifted her face towards her own. Her mother's hands were rough, like the bark of a tree, but they felt like the only bit of happiness that was left for Shandoah to hold on to. Her mother had stayed. She was the only one who had not turned her back on Shandoah.

"My child," her mother said softly. "Go to the swamps to the south. I have a friend there."

"A friend?" Shandoah couldn't remember her mother ever leaving the forest.

"When I was young, I was full of energy, like you," her mother said. Her hand slid down and took Shandoah's hand in hers. "You get your exuberance from me."

Shandoah managed a half-laugh. She had always wished to be like her mother.

"I ran away for a time when I was young," her mother said.

"You?" Shandoah gasped.

"Yes," her mother nodded. "Your grandfather was even stricter with me, if you can believe it."

Shandoah nodded. She could believe it. Being his daughter had to have higher expectations than being his granddaughter.

"Go find Arrose," her mother said. "She is a water elemental and the queen of the swamps. She will protect you and give you shelter. There are many runaways that find refuge there."

"A water elemental?" Shandoah had heard rumors of the elementals. None of them were good.

"She has a good heart," her mother said. "She takes in those that need homes. The swamp is a refuge."

Shandoah nodded. "I'll find her."

"Tell her you are my daughter," her mother said. "She'll understand."

"You're staying?" Shandoah's eyes filled with tears.

"I have to," her mother said. "It will be me that is needed to fix the spell that has been broken."

"But you'll be all right?" Shandoah asked.

Her mother nodded, choking back tears. "And so will you."

Shandoah threw her arms around her mother. "I'm so sorry."

"I know," her mother said. "Now go. Find Arrose."

Her mother let go of her and took a step back.

Shandoah took one last look at her mother and gave her a weak smile. "I love you."

"I love you too," her mother said. And then she turned her back on Shandoah and disappeared into the forest.

Shandoah choked back the tears once again. The first day of spring had already been forgotten. She had to find Arrose. A water elemental was now her only hope.

Shandoah turned to the south and started to run.

Ragwort

Down by the swamp, there was a thunderous crash. The sound of twisting metal was almost deafening. A lone troll, who was fishing in the swamp's murky water, responded to the noise by searching out its source.

He walked through the fog, his green knuckles dragging on the ground beside him. Up a small hill was a road where he found two automobiles in a tangled, steaming mess. They had knocked down one of the ancient trees by the road and one vehicle was half wrapped around it. The troll looked inside the twisted metal, but could not smell the sweet scent of life anywhere among the humans.

Off to his right, the troll heard some leaves rustle and a twig crack. He lumbered toward the noise. A bush near the top of the fallen tree moved slightly. The troll moved slowly, tentatively, toward the bush. He lifted a large leaf out of the way and underneath was something he had never seen before. The troll let out a small gasp and the creature turned its head at the noise. It had huge blue eyes and almost no hair. It looked human, but it was the smallest human he had ever seen. Plus, unlike the humans he had seen hiking through the hills, this one wore no clothes. Only a strange white material covering its bottom that made a crinkling sound when it moved.

The troll took a step forward to get a better look. The small human's eyes grew larger as the troll leaned forward, and then it did something that startled the troll. It raised its tiny arms and stretched them out, reaching for the large green creature before it.

The troll paused, and then took another step forward and reached out to the tiny bald human. It was so small, the troll could scoop it up with one hand. The troll raised his hand to his face as the tiny human nestled into his palm. The troll turned, still staring at the creature in his hand, and headed back down the hill to the swamp.

Once at the bottom of the hill, the troll wandered to the edge of the water where he had been fishing. He sat down on a nearby stump and continued to stare at the tiny human in his hand.

There was the sound of bubbling in the water in front of him. Small waves lapped at the troll's feet. The bubbling grew louder and the waves larger and more frequent. The troll's attention never parted from the tiny creature that was now peacefully asleep in his hand.

A huge burst of water exploded in the middle of the swamp and a woman in white suddenly appeared standing on the water in front of him. At least, she looked like a woman. She had no definite end to her in the mists of the swamp. She blended perfectly with the mist she generated around her, there was no definition of where her clothing and hair and even where she herself ended and the mist began. She was not human, although most humans might mistake her for one.

The troll, never taking his eyes off the creature in his hand, knew that the water elemental that ruled his swamp was standing before him.

"Kirog," she said, in a voice as soothing as a cool rain. The troll slowly looked up, finally tearing his eyes away from his new prize.

"Kirog, you have taken something that does not belong to you," she said sweetly, as if to a child.

The troll looked back to his hand and the sleeping creature.

"W-wh-what is it?" Kirog whispered.

"You have found a human infant," she said.

"You mean a baby?"

"Yes, Kirog, she's a baby. But that means her parents will come looking for her."

"Parents are dead," he said, thinking of the bodies in the steaming, twisted metal.

"Then they will send a search party to retrieve the infant. We are not safe with her here."

Kirog looked at the baby in his hand and sighed.

"Want to keep her," he demanded.

The water elemental suppressed a smile. "It is too dangerous to keep her."

"But she like me." Kirog looked closer at the sleeping infant and took a small sniff. He wrinkled his nose and added, "And she smell funny."

The water elemental looked at him. At over 10 feet tall, trolls were one of the strongest and most dangerous creatures in the swamp. But Kirog was different. He was sweeter and gentler than almost every Fae she had known in her lifetime. A lifetime that spanned thousands of years. Kirog was abandoned when he was just an infant himself, considered to be too stupid, even by troll standards, to be able to survive. She had taken pity on him and raised him as her own. She taught him the ways of the swamp, and even to speak. A feat that was beyond most trolls.

Now, seeing him holding a human infant, abandoned in the swamp, it was no wonder he felt the need to care for the child. Kirog cared for many injured creatures in the swamp, but she could see a love in his eyes that could not match any feelings he had for any other creature. The infant was so small, she fit in the cup of the huge troll's hand. He had barely taken his eyes off her, watching her every breath with fascination.

She was glad Kirog had learned quickly not to poke at small injured creatures. There was an incident with an otter in the past that she did not wish to see repeated. Kirog had sobbed for days, never letting go of the tiny otter. It had taken her sometime to help him get over the fact that he was the cause of the accidental tragedy.

"Kirog," she said gently.

He raised just his eyes to look at her, keeping his face aimed at the sleeping baby.

"You can care for her until the humans come to find her."

"Want to keep her," he insisted, looking back at the infant.

"You know humans in the swamp are dangerous for us. She must be returned to them when they come."

"Want to keep her!" he insisted louder.

The baby opened her eyes wide at the sound of his voice and started to cry. Kirog pulled his hand close to his chest and made shushing noises while slowly rocking his hand back and forth.

Arrose watched as he calmly spoke to her, in a quiet voice, and rocked her back to sleep.

"You may keep her until the humans come," she said firmly.

"Ragwort," he said.

"What?" the elemental asked, surprised by the sudden shift in conversation.

"Her name Ragwort."

Arrose laughed, "You can't name her Ragwort."

"My favorite plant, Ragwort."

"That's hardly a name fit for a little girl."

"Ragwort pretty. She pretty. Ragwort."

Arrose looked around her and saw the water lilies floating at her feet.

"How about Lily? That's a name much more suited for a human girl."

Kirog was silent for a moment as he considered this.

"Lily Ragwort," he said firmly.

Arrose sighed and smiled again, knowing that was the best she would get out of him. "Lily Ragwort is a lovely name."

A short time later, the swamp was lit up by the flickering blue and red lights from police cars. Kirog sat quietly, with Lily gently cupped in his hand. He watched from a hidden vantage point, waiting to see if the humans would search for Lily. He was reluctant to give her up, but had conceded to Arrose that the best place for Lily to grow up would be with other humans.

Kirog watched as a crew of men came to take away the bodies of the people in the crushed automobiles. Policemen in their uniforms measured the ground and scribbled notes on to cards held in their hands. Another crew of men came and put the twisted frames of the cars up on to the back of even larger flatbed trucks. The swamp echoed with the beeping of the trucks and the grinding of chains. The policemen spoke to one another as the cars were towed away, and all the while, Kirog waited for the search to begin. He was to leave Lily in plain sight if they began the search.

The uniformed men pointed at the tree that had fallen. Kirog sucked in his breath and held it as all the men looked straight at the bush he had found Lily under. After another short conversation, the men got into their cars and drove off, leaving the swamp in the fading light of sunset. The troll let out his breath in a sigh of relief.

"They gone, little Ragwort. I keep you now," he whispered to the now stirring baby.

Lily looked up into Kirog's gentle loving eyes, and started to cry.

More books by Judy Lunsford:

Gamers
Schemers

Fire Lily
Bezbell
Kirog

Moonlight Magic
Moonlight Melody

The Red Dart
Shadow Mountain

The Portal Wars
The Grimoires

Short Story Collections:
The Dark of Night
Fairy Short Stories
Fairy Tales & Nightmares
Fantasy Faire
First Stories
Magic from the Dark
Story Hoard
The Wild Hunt

Thank you for reading.
If you enjoyed this book, you can find more stories
at
JudyLunsford.com
or your favorite online retailer.
